The Horrors of Rejection

A Collection of Rejected Short Stories

Radar DeBoard

Contents

IMPORTANT NOTE ABOUT THESE STORIES!

Each and every one of these stories was rejected at least once. Hell, sometimes they were rejected nearly half a dozen times by several different publishers. And you know what? That's totally okay because that's a huge part of being a writer. It doesn't matter how far you come in improving your craft, or how big of a name you become, you're going to get rejected. That rejection does not make you a bad writer. It certainly doesn't mean you are not good enough and need to quit. Sometimes things just don't go your way. That's what happened to me with each of these stories.

The reasons for why my stories have been rejected are numerous and make up an ever-growing list. Some didn't match the theme of the open call, others just barely missed the cut among hundreds of submissions, and some...some did not need to see the light of day because they sucked. I'll admit, each rejection stung, and as you read this collection, you'll see I've had a lot of them. But I never let that stop me. And you shouldn't let that stop you either. Regardless of what you are doing, whether it's writing or not, rejection is going to be a part of it. Don't let that stop you from doing what you love to do. Hopefully the over dozen examples of mine you are about to read will show you that rejection is nothing more than a part of life. Embrace it. Learn from it. And use it to take what you are doing to the next level!

Matthew Gillgack and the Oversized Sack

Many years ago in the

town of Lagnome

It was the perfect place

for anyone to call

home

Everyone was happy

and filled with glee

"Chirp," went all the

birds and "buzz,"
went all the bees
Yet, far away on the
outskirts of town
There was one man
who always wore a
frown
Living all alone in a
rundown, old shack
Was the terrifying
Matthew Gillgack
An individual who
had never heard of
personal hygiene
Not to mention, he
was constantly saying
something obscene
Wherever he went, he
brought diseases and
flies
Never before had one
man been so despised
Unnerving people,
that was Matthew's
knack

Especially, when he

had his enormous sack

That sack was two feet

wide and six feet long

And made of strange

material that was in-

credibly strong

People would ask,

"Hey Matthew,

what's in the sack?"

Then Matthew would

chuckle, "I'll show

you for a snack."

Of course, no one ever

did give him food

Plain and simple, he

was just too rude

It would take the po-

lice getting involved

For the sack's mystery

to finally be solved

For it was during a

pitch-black night

That Officer MacBer-

ry witnessed a horrify-

ing sight
For Macberry was pa-
trolling his usual street
When he saw Gillgack

shuffling his feet
Then Macberry no-
ticed something dif-
ferent about Gill-

gack's bag
It was so full that Gill-
gack was letting it drag
Macberry had to ask,
there was no fighting
it back
So he went,
"Matthew, what's in
the sack?"
Gillgack just smiled
and pulled out a newly
severed head
While Macberry
screamed out, "My
god! They're dead!"
Unfortunately, no
one was around to

hear Macberry's cries
As Gillgack took a
spoon and scooped
out his eyes
Then just like that,
Gillgack was gone in a
flash
Ran out of the town
with a quick little dash
Ever since that night,
everyone in town
has kept their doors
locked
They hid in their
houses with their
double barrels cocked
For they all dread
the return of Matthew
Gillgack
And more than that,
they fear they'll end
up in his sack

Show Some Teeth

Margarette looked away from the computer monitor to give her eyes a moment's rest. She peered out the window and noticed a large crow sitting on the tree branch nearly directly in line with her eyes. Margarette couldn't put her finger on it, but something was off about the bird. It seemed to be staring right at her. The creature didn't flap its wings or adjust itself on the branch, it just simply sat there and stared at her. She saw the bird start to open its beak ever so slowly, and from the small opening, she could have sworn she saw something white inside.

"Margarette!" an angry voice suddenly growled.

She whipped her head away from the window to see Mr. Danvers standing at the entrance to her cubicle with his arms crossed. "Y-yes, Mr. Danvers?" she replied quietly.

"What are you doing, daydreaming?"

"No, I-" she started to say, but was cut off.

"I would hope not," Danvers scowled at her. "Especially not when I asked you to get those revenue reports done by eleven."

"I-I'm almost finished with them now, sir," she stuttered. "Y-you should have them in the next thirty minutes."

"I'd better," he said narrowing his eyes. He put an arm on the top of the cubical wall and sighed, "You know what you are, Margarette?"

"What, sir?"

"A slacker!" Danvers yelled. "Not only are you a slacker, but you're weak. You don't have any backbone; you can't stand up for yourself. That's why everyone in here can pawn their work off on you... because you won't say no. You've infected them all with your bad personality." He leaned in towards Margarette and lowered his voice. "I would have fired you months ago if it weren't for the fact that you can type up a damn fine report." He shook his head, "I'll tell you what, if you don't start standing up for yourself—you know, show some teeth—you're outta here!"

With that Danvers walked away, leaving Margarette to feel sorry for herself. She fought back a few tears as she turned towards her monitor. Now she had thirty minutes to finish something that would probably take her another hour. She knew Mr. Danvers had been after her for a long time, trying to find a legitimate excuse to fire her, but now he might actually get one. There was no way she was going to be able to type up all those reports by the time he wanted them, and he knew it. She was going to get canned.

Margarette felt the hairs on the back of her neck stand up as the unpleasant sensation of being watched traveled up her spine. She slowly turned her gaze back to the window and noticed a second crow was now sitting next to the first. The two sat on the branch in the exact same way, neither one moving or adjusting at all, and both seemed to look directly at her. The first crow slowly began to open its beak bit by bit. She let out a gasp as she saw that the bird had a set of teeth. Not just any kind of teeth, but they seemed to be human teeth.

"Are you okay?" a concerned voice asked.

Margarette jumped a little and turned to see Daniel peeking over the top of his cubicle. She sighed. "Yeah, I guess... I'm as good as I can be."

"I can't believe you let him treat you like that," Daniel shook his head. "He's such a dick to you. You need to stand up to him."

Margarette frowned. "He's my boss. I can't do that, he'll fire me."

"Well, it sounds like he wants to fire you anyway," Daniel commented. He sighed, "You've gotta show some teeth, Margarette. Everyone else in the office has been pushing you around for too long." He checked behind him then whispered, "I told off Stacy for you. Now you don't have to handle her weekly shipment reports."

"Oh, Danny," she smiled. "Thank you. I really appreciate it."

Daniel nodded, "No problem. Anything to help out a friend." He smiled. "Just let me know if you need anything else."

Margarette watched Daniel's head disappear from her view before turning back towards her computer. She took a deep breath and then focused on the task at hand. Margarette immediately found her groove and started to type away, making a huge dent in the reports. As she was finishing up her sixth report, that familiar and uneasy sensation crept up on her again. She couldn't help but glance back at the window, where she spotted almost a dozen crows now perched on the same tree branch. The one with the human teeth in its beak seemed to be smiling at her and a sense of panic bubbled up in her gut. She watched as the bird next to the crow with human teeth opened its beak to present a set of razor-sharp fangs.

Margarette jumped out of her seat and let out a little scream before running around into Daniel's cubicle. "Daniel!" she frantically whispered.

"What's wrong?" he asked with clear concern.

"The birds," Margarette stuttered. "Something's wrong with the birds at my window."

"The birds?" Daniel repeated in confusion. He stood up and walked over to Margarette's cubicle. He looked at the row of crows that were sitting on the tree branch in front of the window but didn't see anything else out of the ordinary. He nodded, "I can see how that could weird you out a bit with them all sitting there like that," Daniel gave a small smile as he turned to look at Margarette, "but it's nothing to get all worked up about. They're just birds."

Margarette looked at the crows and blinked a few times. They didn't seem to be abnormal at the moment. She took a deep breath to calm herself and then nodded. "I guess you're right, Daniel," she shook her head. "I-It must be the stress of this deadline. I guess it has me seeing things." She smiled. "Thanks for putting up with me."

Daniel shrugged. "We've all been there. Last week, I swore I saw Bigfoot walk into the breakroom." He chuckled, "Turns out it was just Tom."

Margarette gave a small giggle. "So I'm not the only one who thinks that."

"No, you're not." Daniel smiled, then slowly said, "Well... I'll uh... let you get back to it." He gave an awkward head nod before returning to his cubicle.

Margarette sat back down in her office chair and tried to get her head into the right space. She started furiously typing up the last report and was making some good progress on it. Margarette checked the time and saw that she only had a few minutes left to send it to Mr. Danvers. There would be no time for her to do any editing like she normally did. She quickly finished the last bit of the report, then typed up an email and sent it over to Mr. Danvers. Margarette let out a deep sigh as she realized it would probably be her last email before she lost her job.

A sudden thud brought her attention away from the computer screen and towards the window once more. She looked at the crows on the tree branch before checking to see what could have made that noise. After several moments of searching, Margarette was about to give up when she saw movement out of the corner of her eye. She looked just in time to see a ball of feathers slam directly into the glass. An audible gasp escaped her lips as the bird fell out of her view towards the ground below.

Margarette brought her gaze back up to the other crows on the tree, and found them sitting perfectly still. She caught some movement above the already-filled branch and lifted her gaze to see several additional birds comfortably perched in another part of the tree. Despite how ridiculous she knew the thought racing through her mind was, she couldn't help but feel all their eyes were deliberately staring at her. She began taking in jagged breaths as her anxiety started to rise. Panic welled up inside as her eyes frantically moved over each crow. Another bird flew off a branch and charged straight at the window. She gasped and jumped a little as the animal slammed into the glass.

She couldn't help but watch as that crow fell to the ground like the one before it. Margarette noticed that a small crack had started to form in the glass thanks to the birds throwing themselves against it. A sinking terror filled her stomach as the idea that the animals were trying to get inside popped into her head. Several of the birds opened their mouths to show off their unsettling, sharp teeth. Her stomach twisted at the thought of being torn apart by the dozens of creatures now perched only a few feet from her.

Margarette shakily stood up from her chair and slowly backed out of her cubicle. Another crow flew into the glass, hitting the exact same spot as the others, and she whirled around to run away. She only took a few steps before she ran straight into Mr. Danvers. He glared at her with an angry look on his face. Margarette didn't care about his fury for once, she was solely focused on getting as far away from the window as possible. She couldn't take hearing another crow slam itself against the glass, the very thought of it causing her to tremble in fear.

"The birds, sir!" she whispered in terror.

Danvers looked past Margarette at the window and saw nothing out of the ordinary except for a crack in the glass. "Margarette, I'm so sick and tired of your stupid attempts to get out of doing work," he hissed. "There aren't even any birds there, you pathetic waste of space."

Margarette snapped her head to the window and found that all the animals had disappeared. She stared in disbelief for several moments and then stuttered, "There were dozens of them." Margarette turned and looked into Mr. Danvers' eyes, "They were here just a minute ago."

"That's it!" Danvers yelled, "I've had it with this crap!" He grabbed Margarette by the left arm and started to drag her off. "You've really screwed the pooch now."

"Hey!" Daniel hollered after them, "Let her go."

"What was that?" Danvers sneered as he turned to look back at Daniel. "Did you want to say something to me?"

"Yes, I do," Daniel said with confidence. "You always treat her like trash. I've had enough of it."

Danvers chuckled, "Oh really? Do you want to trade places with this deadweight?" Silence followed his question and he shook his head. "I didn't think so." He hissed at Daniel, "Get back to work."

Margarette watched as Daniel reluctantly turned and shuffled back into his cubicle. Meanwhile, Danvers tightened his grip on her wrist enough to start hurting her. He dragged Margarette past all her coworkers, making sure they all could see the display as a way to further heighten her humiliation. Danvers took them to his office and slammed the door. He finally let go of her and aggressively pointed at the lone office chair placed in front of his desk. She sat down quietly as Danvers looked at her with disgust.

After a moment of silence, Danvers finally spoke up. "I took a look at the revenue reports you sent me." He shook his head. "That was the one thing you had going for you, Margarette. The one thing you had, and you screwed it up so badly that you made me look like an idiot!" Danvers pounded his fist on his desk, "I've never seen anything so poorly written in my life! Not to mention, you sent it to me five minutes after eleven."

"Y-you gave me an impossible task," Margarette quietly stuttered.

"What was that, Stuttering Sally?" Danvers said mockingly. "I couldn't hear you because you're quieter than a fart from a church mouse. Makes it easy to sneak off and not do your work, huh?"

"I always do my work, sir," Margarette said, with tears starting to form in her eyes.

"Cut the crap!" Danvers screamed. "I know you haven't been doing your work for a long time. And even when you actually get it done, it's garbage!" He chuckled. "I think you know what comes next."

"Please don't, sir," Margarette whimpered.

The feeling of something watching her drew Margarette's gaze to the window, where she saw a crow perched on a tree limb. The bird was staring directly at her as it opened its beak to reveal its human teeth. She felt a sense of panic start to overpower her other emotions.

"What the hell are you staring at?" Danvers yelled.

"The crow!" Margarette said, pointing at the window.

"There you go talking about birds again." Danvers rolled his eyes at her. "I don't know what game you're trying to play, but it won't work. It's clear you're too busy paying attention to the wildlife to do your job." Danvers took in a deep breath. "So, you're fired!"

Margarette looked away from the dozen or so crows that had just landed on the perch and stared into Mr. Danvers' eyes. "You can't do this to me," she pleaded. "I-I need this job."

"Everybody needs a job," Danvers growled. "Maybe you should have thought about having a better work ethic before now."

"How?" she asked as she started to cry. "I'm in here before anyone else, and I'm one of the last to leave." Margarette shook her head, "I put in more hours than you!"

"Don't try to talk yourself up with some lies," Danvers sneered. "I know you goof around in your cubicle all day instead of working."

"How could you possibly know that?" Margarette asked as a small bit of anger started to bubble up in her voice. She heard a thudding sound against the window and proceeded to ignore it. "Unless you watched me every hour of every single day, you would have no way of knowing if I'm goofing off or not."

Danvers waved his finger at Margarette. "You're not the first person to use that argument on me. I can tell who's a hard worker and who isn't. And let me tell you, you're not a hard worker." He slowly stood up. "The only thing I've ever seen you do that was worth a damn is your reports. Other than that, you can't do anything else correctly. You're one of the dumbest people I have ever met! Hell, I don't even know how you got this job! You must have lied your way through the interview. Hell, maybe you banged the right person; that would make sense."

Several thumping sounds came against the glass and Margarette looked to see a crack forming on the window. She didn't care though. After years of abuse from her boss, he had finally gone too far by insulting her intelligence and her morals.

Margarette screamed back, "Shut up you disgusting, worthless shell of a man! All you do is berate other people for not doing their jobs, but it's clear that you don't do yours. Those revenue reports are your responsibility, yet you threw them on me." She stood up to look Danvers in the eye. "You're the one who's dumb and incompetent! You treat everyone around you like crap because you're a worthless human being." She jammed a finger into his chest as she yelled, "Screw you!"

The glass of the window suddenly shattered as dozens of crows filled the room. Margarette and Danvers both screamed in horror as the animals flew around them. The birds circled for several seconds before swooping down on top of her boss. Margarette tripped over her own feet trying to step backwards and fell to the ground. She watched in terror as the crows swarmed Danvers and started ripping into him with their sharp teeth. Gripped with fear, she could only watch as chunks of her boss' flesh were ripped off him.

"Help me!" he screamed. "Oh god, help me!"

Margarette sat on the ground, completely stunned by what she was witnessing. The animals continued their feast on Danvers while he screamed in agony. Margarette noticed one of the crows pecking at Danvers' left eye. Blood oozed out of the socket as the man tried to scramble around his desk, while also swatting at the birds. The blood-soaked victim tripped and fell just a few feet from her. She quickly scrambled back in fear of the crows taking an interest in her as well. Margarette scooted away from the carnage until her back hit the wall.

There was nothing she could do but watch the horrifying and unnatural teeth of the crows as they continued to bite into Danvers. He finally stopped flailing and looked at Margarette with his one eye. She saw him take his last breath as the birds continued their feast. There was no doubt in her mind that they would pick his bones clean in a matter of minutes with how fast they were going. Margarette wanted more than anything to flee the room but was far too afraid of the birds to make a move. Another crow flew through the window and softly landed on her knee. She sat completely still while trying to keep from crying as the animal studied her. It opened its beak to show her that it was the one with human teeth.

In an almost human voice, the crow cawed, "Show some teeth."

Margarette sat in stunned horror, unable to comprehend what she had just heard.

The crow turned its head and stared at her as it said, "'Show some teeth,' he said. Well, we showed him our teeth instead."

From a Bathtub to the Ocean

THE WOODEN LIFEBOAT WAS no match for the monstrous waves of the ocean. Jerome could easily hear the creaking of the boards under the strain of the sea slapping against them. It was only a matter of time before something broke and water started to flood in around him. More likely than not, he wouldn't be able to witness his demise due to the overcast sky blocking any moonlight from reaching him. The only reason anything was visible to him now was the flames coming off the large cargo ship he had abandoned only minutes prior. He was still close enough to hear the crackling of the fire and the screaming of the crew, but he would soon be far enough away that the fire's light would fade.

It seemed that his escape attempt was going to end before it had even truly begun. Sure, he had successfully fled Boston by stowing away on the vessel that was now alight before him, but it had only made it a day or so from shore. They were more than a week's voyage from where the crew had left the harbor for. Perhaps that was a good thing. Jerome had told himself not to meddle in the affairs of the crew that had so graciously agreed to smuggle him out of America for a small fee, but there were disturbing details that he picked up on. The hundreds of manacles and chains, combined with an absurdly cramped area of additional sleeping quarters that the sailors themselves did not partake in, told him exactly what the crew was aiming to smuggle. A part of him was thankful they did not reach their destination since that meant he had avoided bearing witness to such a deplorable and disgusting trade. At the very least, his hands were clean on that front.

As for the deaths of the smugglers themselves, that fell squarely on his shoulders. After all, he was the one who started the fire. Not intentionally of course, but his hands were the ones that tossed the lantern which would engulf the sleeping quarters in flames. He was just trying to stop that horrendous thing from reaching him. That inhuman creature had been following him since he had gone on the lamb. It had been whispering to him, putting his mind on edge and depriving him of much-needed sleep. Of course, his body betrayed him when the supernatural thing finally revealed itself. As sleep deprived as he was, how could it have not? Whether he meant to start the fire or not, that didn't matter to the crew. They would burn to death and the ones that escaped from a fiery doom would drown, as he had commandeered the sole lifeboat for himself.

Now that he was alone on the vastness of the ocean, he waited to see what would come first: the authorities or a leak. However, he was taken by surprise when a hand shot out of the water and grabbed ahold of the side of the lifeboat. The drenched limb pulled a bloated and water-logged body from the waves, delivering it onto the oppo-site end of the boat from him. With the light from the burning ship becoming a dim glow in the distance, it took him several moments, but he finally managed to identify the rotting corpse of his wife.

Her spirit had managed to break free from its final rest-ing place in the lone bathtub of their apartment and had followed him out to sea. She had been the one polluting his mind and driving his hand to commit such a large mistake. It was all to get him alone, truly alone on the open water, so that she could take what was hers. Vengeance would be oh-so-sweet, especially since Jerome's screams for help had no hope of bringing him salvation.

Immurement

Thomas desperately slid his hands against the bricked-off surface, feeling for some imperfection or crack. His fingers frantically searched every crevice in place of his eyes, which were utterly useless in the pitch-black darkness. Constant droplets of sweat poured down from Thomas' brow thanks to the ever-rising temperature in the sealed-off area he found himself trapped in. Each time Thomas moved it seemed as though the space got a tad bit hotter.

After scouring every inch of the bricked wall in front of him to no avail, Thomas let out a pathetic whimper before slumping to the floor. He tried to take a deep breath to calm down, but the air was musty and he ended up furiously coughing instead. The closed walls echoed the sounds of his coughs back at him, hurting his ears from the amplified noise. His coughs turned into sobs as the true hopelessness of his situation finally washed over him. The air around him tasted of dirt and death, with the flavor growing ever stronger after each breath. He knew it wouldn't be long before the supply of oxygen ran out, a thought which caused him to sob even harder.

Thomas continued to weep over his approaching demise as his mind replayed past memories of his life. He went through all his loved ones in his head, trying to think how all of them would react to his death. As Thomas thought about those he'd be leaving behind, his brother naturally floated into his brain. He wondered if what he was going through now was how his brother felt in his last moments. The thought of his little brother gasping for air while trapped in an enclosed space with no one there to help him suddenly lit a seething rage inside of Thomas.

He scrambled to his feet and began to kick at the wall with all the fury he could muster. Thomas' shoes harmlessly bounced off the brick, but he continued to strike the wall before him. The frustration of not being able to break out of his tomb only added to his anger, pushing him to the point where he started to punch the brick. Thomas' hands immediately flared with agony upon the first hit, but his raw emotion overpowered his common sense and he kept punching.

Thomas continued until he felt something break in his left hand, as a wave of agony simultaneously shot up his arm. He couldn't help but let out a kneejerk roar of pain before furiously kicking the wall with his right leg. Thomas continued to do so until a similar sensation of agony engulfed his foot, causing him to stumble backward. He couldn't maintain his balance and fell, slamming his head against the back wall of his tomb. The hit caused his mind to lose clarity, and the boy fell over on the floor, his limbs flopping against the ground.

"I just wanted to find Jake," Thomas mumbled weakly.

His mind randomly thought back to Mr. Sowers asking, "Thomas... do you know what immurement is?"

Thomas spat in disgust at the recollected words of his horrific neighbor. The man was a monster that had managed to fool everyone. All the years of missing children, heartbroken parents, and sleepless nights lying awake in fear, were because of Mr. Sowers. Thomas felt his mind start to drift towards unconsciousness and he couldn't seem to fight it, try as he might. His eyes lazily drifted towards the wall before him where he happened to notice a small beam of light shining through. Thomas gasped in surprise as his muddled mind managed to understand that he had done just enough to loosen one of the bricks in the wall. It was a final moment of hope that Thomas tried to cling to as his mind seemed to automatically power down.

"I'm coming, Jake," Thomas mumbled incoherently as he drifted off into unconsciousness.

Durable Tires

JOSEPH PAUSED FOR A moment in hesitation as he gazed up at the worn-down, yellow sign that simply read *Great Tires*. Though Alek had recommended the spot to him, Joseph was starting to have doubts about his longtime friend's referral. The place was already located in a rather sketchy part of town, but the fact that it was tucked behind a foreclosed strip mall had him considering just leaving. He contemplated what he should do for a few more seconds before remembering that his car had been towed there, and with two blown-out tires, he only had one real option. Joseph slowly let out a defeated sigh and gingerly pushed open the glass door to enter the tire store.

The first thing that he noticed was the rather peculiar odor that permeated the air. The scent of tire rubber encircled him as would be expected, but there was something else with it, a horrific stench that managed to hide itself within the scent of rubber. Joseph wracked his brain for something that could describe what his nose was picking up, but all he could muster was the word 'rotten', as though some large animal had managed to crawl into the tire shop and die without anyone being aware of it.

Joseph's thoughts on the horrible odor were interrupted by someone asking in a sharp tone, "What do you want?"

He brought his attention to the small counter, only twenty or so feet from where he currently was, and spotted a short woman, around five foot two, shooting him a suspicious look. It took Joseph a moment to process the question, but once he had, he immediately headed for the counter. As he approached, Joseph was able to identify the unfortunate bowl cut the short woman wore, along with a clunky pair of thick-rimmed glasses that magnified her eyes just enough to make them seem unnaturally large. He came to a stop just in front of the area where she stood, which was also occupied by an outdated cash register.

Before Joseph could speak, the woman bluntly asked again, "What do you want?"

A thick, European accent of some sort was much easier to detect now that Joseph was close enough to hear what the short woman was saying. He took but a few seconds to ponder what country the accent could have come from before he realized that the woman was quickly growing impatient.

"I'm here to get some tires put on my car," he finally replied.

The woman narrowed her eyes and then pointed an accusing finger at him. "So you're the one who dropped their car off here without calling," she growled. "Do you have any manners? To simply park a car somewhere with no notice... it's disgraceful!"

"I... I know," Joseph quickly tried to apologize. "I wouldn't normally do it, but Alek recommended..."

"Alek!" the abrasive lady suddenly shouted in surprise. Her magnified eyes grew a little larger as she said, "Why didn't you just say so?" She began to search for something just out of Joseph's view while saying, "I am Ksenia, the owner of this store." Ksenia finally found what she was looking for and loudly slapped it onto the counter.

Joseph stared down at the item placed before him, which was a small and worn-down, black notebook. He was confused as to why Ksenia had retrieved the notebook until the short woman produced a pen from her pocket. She clicked it several times too many before spending a few seconds forcefully rubbing the pen against the journal's open pages. After an awkward moment of silence, ink finally began to appear on the page, and she glanced up at Joseph with a small nod of her head.

There were a few seconds of silence that followed, in which it became apparent that Ksenia was growing even more annoyed. She asked with a loud sigh, "What tires?"

"What... tires?" Joseph responded in confusion to the vague question.

Ksenia rolled her eyes, then rephrased the question. "What kind of tires do you need, and how many?"

"Uh... well, two of them are flat... so, I guess uh... I'll probably need four," Joseph slowly responded while trying to search his brain for any helpful detail about his car's tires. "Um... what kind of tires," he muttered to himself. "That's... that's a good question." Joseph hesitated for a moment before admitting, "I-I honestly don't know what kind of tire."

Ksenia scowled at him for several minutes then let out a heavy sigh as she moved out from around the counter. "I guess that's okay," she grumbled. "We have your car, so we can take a look to see what you need."

Joseph instinctively started to follow Ksenia, as he thought she was going to show something of importance to him. Instead, the short woman whirled around and snapped at him.

"You wait up here!" she growled, while angrily gesturing to a set of worn chairs made of grey plastic and rusting metal. An awkward pause circled in the air and then Ksenia changed her tone to sound more hospitable as she explained, "We'll take care of everything ourselves. You just relax and wait. It will all be ready shortly."

"O-Okay then," Joseph replied with a clear lack of confidence in his voice.

"Don't..." Ksenia suddenly said at a volume close to a yell, before quickly lowering it once again, "try to follow me. The workers can be a little... reckless at times." She shot Joseph a large grin that he could tell was forced as she added, "I wouldn't want you to get hurt."

Joseph slowly nodded as he watched the strange woman gradually back up, still staring at him. Finally, she turned around and headed to a set of steps that were located at the back left corner of the room. Joseph listened to the sounds of her shoes thumping against each step as Ksenia forcefully descended the stairs. After a minute, the footsteps stopped, and Joseph could hear the sound of a heavy door being pulled open.

At that moment, the faint smell of rot that had been hanging in the air grew exponentially in strength. He couldn't help but gasp in disgust, quickly plugging his nose. Seconds later, Joseph heard the door Ksenia had opened being slammed shut. He cautiously kept his nose plugged for several more minutes before finally taking a chance and unclamping his fingers from around his nostrils.

It didn't take long after that for Joseph's mind to drift from the horrific odor and focus on the feeling of boredom that gradually overwhelmed him. After only ten minutes, he began to question why Ksenia hadn't come back yet. Since she seemed to be in charge of the register and greeting guests, it only made sense that she wouldn't leave her post for too long. Yet, with each minute that slowly ticked by, it seemed more and more unlikely that Ksenia was going to stomp her way back up the stairs. Joseph began to feel like he had been forgotten. He felt like the store owner had just told him what he wanted to hear to keep him amiable while she completely ignored Joseph and kept him waiting as long as possible.

After forty minutes, he finally had enough. A growing anger bubbled up as he stood to his feet, kicking the uncomfortable chair he had been sitting on in the process. Joseph stomped across the floor at a fast pace towards the steps he had seen Ksenia descend almost an hour prior. He reached the top of the steps and hesitated for a brief moment as he peered down. The first thing that caught his eye was the fact that the steps went further down than he would have thought possible. With a great deal of effort, he tried to find where the stairs ended, but thanks to an absence of light, the steps seemed to vanish into darkness about halfway down.

The growing anger that he had been feeling quickly dissipated and was fast replaced with the strong pull of fear. He had no desire to tentatively make his way into darkness just for the opportunity to yell at someone for their abysmal customer service. It certainly wasn't worth the potential tumble down the dozens of concrete steps. Joseph turned back in the direction of the sections of chairs where he had been sitting, but as he did, a muffled scream reached his ears. Now, curiosity had fought its way into contention with the other emotions battling against each other inside him. He couldn't help but bring his gaze back towards the steps while remaining as still as possible, in an attempt to hear any more noises that might arise. Only a few seconds passed before another, faint scream made its way to him.

Sure, the sound was no louder than a whisper, but Joseph was certain it was a human shriek. That small confirmation was all it took to drive his curiosity to the forefront of all other emotions. He immediately began making his way down the stairs at a brisk pace. After the first dozen or so steps, he dramatically slowed down the tempo, finding it harder to identify where he should step with the decreasing amount of natural light. Joseph pulled his cell phone from his pocket and flipped on the flashlight app that came pre-downloaded onto the device before continuing downward.

After a few more steps, he heard another scream that was slightly louder than the first two. Though it was brief, he was able to pick up more details about the mysterious cry. He could hear the terror embedded within the shriek, which sent a chill up his spine. Joseph shuddered, then took the next twenty or so steps with a somewhat faster pace, driven forth by the burning curiosity to uncover the mystery behind the shrieks coming from the dark. Several more of the screams sounded as he continued his descent, each one growing louder and revealing more to him.

By the time Joseph reached the final step, he had concluded that someone was terrified, and more importantly, in great amounts of pain. He shined the light from his cell phone and found a narrow corridor laid out before him. There was but a single door at the end of the hallway, giving him no other choice than to cautiously move forward. He took his time, taking each step with the utmost care, so as not to alert whoever was causing the screams of agony to his presence. Once he had finally reached the door, he took hold of the rounded knob, and oh so gently tried to turn it. To his surprise, he felt the knob turn all the way, and he cracked the door open so that a small gap formed.

A beam of dim light forced its way through the opening, illuminating the hallway just enough to give him some peace of mind. He proceeded to turn off his phone's flashlight and then tucked it back in his pocket. Joseph braced himself as he mentally prepared to open the door further, but before he could, his ears picked up the sound of something moving. Instinctively, he sucked in his breath while pressing his body against the sliver of the wall to the left of the doorframe. He focused all his attention on the small opening, desperately hoping that whatever was moving about just behind the door would not see the gap.

"That's still not enough," a man with a slight Eastern European accent grumbled.

A familiar voice responded, "How is that possible? I have cut off more than enough for you to work with."

"Cut off?" Joseph mouthed to himself in confusion as he slid forward just a few more inches towards the doorframe.

"These tires are much bigger than the ones we usually make," the first voice replied swiftly. "There is much more material that must be altered at once."

"You're just being lazy!" shouted the second voice, which sounded all too familiar to Joseph.

It took him a bit longer than it should have, but he was eventually able to identify that Ksenia was the one who was shouting. A sudden shriek of agony cut through the air, and Joseph took advantage by gently pushing the door open by a few more centimeters. He moved in closer towards the door and was able to see several dozen candles littering the space off to the right side of the room. A large amount of flame would normally set off an internal alarm inside of him, but his attention quickly became occupied with a puddle of red liquid that he could just barely see spreading out across the ground.

"Oh wow," the unidentified voice said in surprised amusement. "He's still alive. I certainly thought he would have bled out after we cut off the right arm."

As soon as those words reached his ears, Joseph felt a crippling dread ripple through his body. His limbs began to violently shake at the thought of what horrible things were being done on the other side of the door he was nearly pressed up against. He tried to step back from the opening as his mind frantically begged him to flee, but his feet refused to move. All he could do was stare at the puddle that he now recognized as blood. The sound of slow-moving footsteps only intensified the terror that froze him in place. After a few moments, Ksenia briefly stepped into his line of sight before moving forward, disappearing from view once more.

"No!" a gurgling voice shrieked out, only thirty or so feet from where Joseph stood.

A ripping noise came from inside the room and was quickly followed by screams of agony. Joseph could clearly hear dripping and tearing sounds nestled in between the wails of unimaginable pain. A queasy feeling erupted from his gut, and he had to fight with all his might not to launch the contents of his stomach out into the world. After what seemed like an unbearably long time, the horrific noises ceased while the cries of agony continued. He couldn't help but let out a horrified gasp as Ksenia once more walked by his line of sight, carrying a severed leg in her right hand that dripped gobs of blood onto the cement ground as she moved.

"Will this be enough?" she asked.

After a pause that seemed to take far too long, the unidentified voice replied, "Probably not."

"Don't play your stupid games with me, Alexandru!" Ksenia shouted in sudden anger.

The voice that Joseph assumed was Alexandru calmly replied, "I'm not. But the tire is going to be very large. The process itself will require a lot. It needs something truly significant to be successful."

"Jesus!" Ksenia exclaimed, "We've got an arm and two legs! What else do we need?"

"Well…" Alexandru paused, then suggested in a tone that resembled a question, "perhaps a head?"

Before Joseph could process what had been said, the sound of Ksenia's footsteps was echoing across the floor.

"No! Jesus! Don't do this!" screamed the unfortunate soul on the opposite side of the door.

A wave of revulsion surged forth inside Joseph's gut, but the power of his curiosity was what made him act. He took the fingertips of his right hand and gently placed them against the door. His limb trembled with fear as he cautiously scooted the door open by another half an inch. Thanks to the constant screams, he was able to widen the gap without being noticed. Now he could see past the pool of blood and was able to spot Ksenia as she conducted her nightmarish work on the doomed man whose entrails were beginning to leak onto the floor. He could hear an unpleasant, gurgling noise escaping from the victim, as the store owner sawed away at the man's neck. Her back was turned in such a way that it blocked Joseph from seeing what was happening, which he was incredibly grateful for.

He tried his hardest not to gag as he witnessed what seemed like gallons of blood spilling onto the floor. Finally, Ksenia let out a loud grunt while performing a ripping motion with her arms, and in the process, tore the head away from the now lifeless body. The eyes of the severed head remained open, and when she started to move to the opposite side of the room, Joseph could have sworn the lifeless body part was looking right at him.

"That's perfect!" Alexandru exclaimed.

The unphased reaction from the man inside the room was the last straw for Joseph. He finally managed to get his feet working, forcing them to move back ever so slowly. It was clear that he needed to report this. He needed to get some help. There was no telling how long these people had been doing whatever the hell he had just witnessed, but it needed to be stopped.

"You shouldn't have come down here," a familiar voice calmly whispered to him.

Before Joseph could react, something hard hit the back of his head and he fell to the ground. He managed to land in such a way that he was pointed at his attacker, and was barely able to see their silhouette. He began to drift in and out of consciousness as the figure moved towards him. His attacker slowly bent down enough to reveal their face.

"Alek?" Joseph mumbled in shock. "W-What are you doing?"

His friend responded by slowly shaking his head. "You just couldn't stay upstairs, could you?"

Joseph tried to respond, but his body failed him as his eyes closed and he was taken into darkness.

***

A loud, humming sound penetrated Joseph's eardrums, ripping him from his unconscious slumber. He instinctively tried to cover his ears but found that he couldn't move his arms fully. Panic gripped him and he frantically turned towards his left arm to see it was shackled. He could tell that his right appendage was also restrained, and he concluded that he had been restrained like the poor, decapitated soul before him. A sudden light, growing at an exponential rate, brought his focus to twenty or so feet in front of him.

Joseph was met by the sight of a man with his hands clasped together, sitting in the middle of a strange emblem that was drawn on the ground. A layer of candles had been periodically placed around the outside of the symbol in a way that added an eeriness to the scene. His eyes eventually honed in on a strange mass lying before the man that seemed to be randomly writhing about. It took a few moments for him to recognize the disembodied head among the several severed appendages, but once he did, he let out a scream of pure terror.

"You're finally awake," Ksenia said with a sinister grin as she walked from somewhere further back in the room.

Joseph paid her no attention, as all his focus was placed on the shaking mass of deceased flesh placed in front of the diligent employee. The humming noise continued to grow louder as the separated body parts moved towards each other. He screamed as loud as possible, not because he expected to be saved, but simply as the only method he had at his disposal to keep his mind from snapping at the horrible display unfolding. The different bits of flesh finally converged and started morphing into something monstrous. Bits of skin and viscera twisted about, while flesh contorted into a circular shape. The shine created by the monstrous process continued to grow in magnitude, while the disgusting mass of flesh started to blacken and patterns began to appear on the outside of the horrific lump.

Several more moments passed, then suddenly, the terrible sound and the intense shine ceased. The mass had seemed to take on the desired form, as the man who had been sitting behind it wore the large grin of a job well done. Joseph stared at the item that was once several different body parts and tried to comprehend how the mass of flesh had been formed into such an object. It was now circular, with a fairly large hole in the middle, while the entire thing had completely blackened. He scanned the obvious patterns that dotted the surface of the object in confusion.

He finally couldn't hold back his voice and he uttered in confusion, "A tire?"

"Not just any tire," Ksenia smirked, "the perfect tire." She pointed at the man still sitting on the ground, "Alexandru is the master of crafting them by using the dark arts."

"Jesus Christ!" Joseph yelled, "You cut up people just to make some tires?"

Alexandru nodded, "We don't have to pay for materials this way. It's a great way to make a lot of profits." He added, "Plus, we only use unsavory characters to make them."

"Like gang members and prostitutes," Ksenia said while taking a large, bladed object from somewhere behind her back. "No one will miss them, and the streets get cleaned up a bit. Everybody wins."

Suddenly, the door to the room swung open, and Alek stepped inside. "We have a new order," he said in a calm and even tone.

Ksenia and Alexandru locked gaze with Joseph while sinister grins spread across their faces.

"Thank goodness we just got some incredible, new material to work with," Ksenia said, taking an eager step towards Joseph. "We might just make our best tires yet."

A Final Present

IN HIS RUSH TO get to the family cabin, he had forgotten his medication. Soon after arriving, the presents under the tree started talking. They told him what to do and with what tools to carry out the tasks. At first, he resisted, progressing through the exercises his doctors had walked him through, but it only worked for a few hours. In the end, he relented, determined to help the wrapped objects save Christmas. One by one his family arrived, coming in from the snow-covered landscape. They barely had time to wipe off their boots before he gave them their gift. The final gift they would ever receive, which they responded to with grunts of agony or screams of terror.

He stacked the bodies next to the fireplace and then waited for the presents' next command, but none came. As the sunlight dissipated, he was left in silence with the festive items. After several hours of waiting for an order, he finally made a decision for himself and approached the fireplace. It wasn't until he lit a fire that he noticed the closed entrance to the crawlspace right next to the wrapped gifts. He lifted the hatch to find a pair of eyes and a grin peeking out from the dark, waiting to deliver his reward for serving them so well.

First Came the Doors

ANDRE NOTICED THE FIRST of the doors on his usual morning jog. He was headed around the lake a few blocks from his house when he looked into one of his neighbor's yards and spotted something peculiar. A large, wooden door with some intricate designs carved into it, stood upright all by itself in the middle of the lawn. What made it particularly peculiar was that the ground was downward sloping towards the lake, making it nearly impossible for an object like a door to keep upright without help. At the time, Andre had thought it a little strange, but hadn't paid it more than a few seconds of his attention. He had continued his jog, leaving the freestanding object just sitting there in his neighbor's yard.

Things become exponentially stranger when he exited his house the next day to find that several of his neighbors had similar doors in their yards. Andre didn't know what to think of the situation, but he certainly found it unsettling. He decided to go examine some of the peculiar items up close, in the hopes that he would be able to figure out what was going on. Andre immediately went for the closest door he could find, which happened to only be three houses down from him. The first thing he noticed about the unusual object as he approached, was that a great deal of detail had been carved into it. Dozens of indents and intersecting lines dotted the wooden surface, creating patterns in the face of the door. As he examined the strange symbols and imagery that had been carved into the wood, his neighbor, Mike, walked outside.

"What the hell are you doing?" Mike asked.

"Nothing," Andre quickly spat out in an uneven tone. He immediately regretted saying anything, as the unconfident response made it seem as though he had done something wrong. "I just noticed this door sitting in the middle of your yard," Andre added.

"Right," Mike slowly said while cautiously moving towards Andre and the door. He gave the object a quick look over before asking, "Did you put this here?"

Andre didn't respond, but simply gestured at the surrounding houses to show that Mike was not alone in his situation.

"So," Mike began with a puzzled expression on his face, "why the hell would someone put this here?"

Andre shrugged. "I have no idea."

Mike stepped in closer and leaned in to examine the door. "Whoever did this, they're one sick puppy." He shook his head. "I mean... this stuff... t-the stuff that's carved in here just isn't right."

Curiosity drove Andre to move closer towards the large piece of freestanding wood. He stared at the carvings in the door for a few seconds but didn't see anything that would elicit the reaction that his neighbor had given. "What are you talking about?" he inquired.

"You don't see it?" Mike responded in surprise. He pointed to one of the carved patterns. "Right there, it's... it's just downright disgusting. I don't want my kids seeing that!"

Complete confusion slammed into Andre as he stared at the place his neighbor was pointing at, only seeing a series of carved squares, connected to each other. "What exactly is it that you're seeing?" he asked.

"Come on, man," Mike said in frustration. "It's right there, you don't need me to describe it to you."

Andre shot Mike a blank stare, which caused his neighbor to realize that they weren't seeing the same thing.

"You really can't see it?" Mike asked with a wavering tone. He looked visibly shaken as he lowered his voice, "T-The face... all twisted and nasty like that. I've never seen something like it... especially with all that... color."

"I... I don't see anything," Andre said in a lowered voice.

"Oh," Mike whispered before suddenly asking, "Do you want to help me get rid of it?"

Andre didn't know what else to do, so he just slowly nodded his head. His neighbor smiled at him and then he placed both hands on the door and pushed against it. To the surprise of both men, the freestanding item didn't immediately topple onto the lawn. The mysterious gift stood tall, clearly causing Mike to become even more unnerved. Andre watched as his neighbor started desperately slamming his body weight against the door, his frantic actions doing nothing to move the object.

"Why won't you move!" Mike shouted.

Andre felt as though he was watching something he shouldn't be and took it upon himself to exit the situation.

He took several steps backward, moving with light trepidation, in part due to the small bit of curiosity that lingered. Mike continued to throw himself against the door, and in turn, the wooden object did not budge a single inch. Andre kept watching as he backtracked towards his own home. It wasn't until he was almost back to his place that he finally turned his gaze away from the spectacle.

As the days went by, more doors began to pop up over the neighborhood. It quickly grew from roughly one out of ten households having a makeshift entrance in the middle of their yards, to over half possessing one in less than seventy-two hours. Andre watched from inside his home as his neighbors examined and prodded the doors, their facial expressions gradually morphing from ones of confusion to those of fear. It was a cycle that repeated itself with the start of a new day. People would wake up and anxiously venture outside to see if they had the misfortune of having a foreign aperture front and center in their yard.

Andre kept thinking back to how Mike had interacted with his door and the way his mood had completely changed in a matter of seconds. More than anything else, curiosity was what truly started to build inside of him. He wanted to find out who had put the doors there, and more importantly, why. Andre changed his schedule so he could stay up at night, carefully watching the perfectly manufactured lawns of the houses around him. The curiosity quickly morphed into an obsession, and he spent his waking moments thinking about the mystery of the doors in the silence of his home.

On the sixth night of his obsessive monitoring, he noticed a bright light coming from Mike's house. Andre was immediately drawn to the strange color of the illumination. It was an indescribable shade of red that he had never seen before, and for some reason, it set a feeling of unease loose in his gut. Andre bounded out of his house, driven by his obsession to understand more about the doors. He gave no thought to social norms as he bounded across his neighbors' yards in nothing but a pair of boxers. Andre glanced towards the light to see that Mike had somehow managed to open the door, which was the origin point of the light.

Andre called out as he approached, "What are you doing?"

"They whisper to me," Mike quietly responded as Andre crossed into his yard.

"What?" Andre inquired as he stopped in confusion.

"Those from beyond the door," Mike answered with a mesmerized gaze on his face. "They've been calling to me for days now," he said with a small chuckle. "I was foolish to think that I could avoid them."

Andre took a few cautious steps toward his neighbor while he calmly said, "You're not making any sense man. Are... are you trying to tell me you've been hearing voices?"

As he moved in a little closer, Andre touched the red light with the tip of his left hand. Immediately after coming into contact with it, Andre was exposed to a horrifying cacophony of wails and screams. He immediately covered his ears to try to muffle the sound, but it didn't seem to have any real effect. The blood-curdling screams continued at full force, making it impossible to hear anything else.

"Jesus Christ!" he yelled. "Can you not hear that?"

Mike simply nodded with a smile spread across his face. Andre struggled forward for a few more steps before dropping to his knees due to the horrifying wails growing ever louder. He struggled to raise his gaze to his neighbor's face, but he was eventually able to. Andre was met by the tear-filled eyes of a man who had accepted his fate, and it created a nauseous feeling along with it. Another small nod was all Mike gave, before he stepped through the doorway and into the epicenter of the otherworldly, red light. A split second after Mike had gone through the door, it disappeared, leaving Andre alone on another man's lawn with nothing to light the night but the moon and a few stars.

Andre scrambled to his feet and sprinted back to his house, slamming the door shut the moment he was inside. He boarded up his windows, taking every precaution to make sure whatever was going on outside wouldn't reach him. Then he proceeded to curl into a ball in the corner of his living room, shaking uncontrollably and trying to understand what he had witnessed. He ended up falling asleep in that spot, spending the night tormented by horrifying visions. Indescribable creatures filled his nightmares, interspliced with scenes of horrible acts being performed on humans.

By the time Andre woke the next morning, his sanity was in a precarious state. He trembled in fear as he crawled from the space by the wall that had been his makeshift bed. Andre cautiously climbed to his feet with a sinking feeling tugging at his gut; it whispered to him, telling him that something was waiting for him. His fears would quickly be confirmed as he moved over to the front window and spied a white door standing in the middle of his yard. He completely froze, unable to do anything for the next hour but stare at the hellish gateway that had been set out for him.

Andre's mind finally forced the rest of his body into action by moving to the bedroom. His limbs quickly maneuvered around the room, throwing various clothes and toiletries into an open suitcase. Andre zipped up the luggage and sprinted through his house, wishing to spend as little time as possible around the door that sat in his yard. He started up his car and prepared to zoom backward down his driveway; yet, a force that was not his own made his hand move. Andre gasped as his limb moved, without any direction from his mind, and turned off the vehicle. He sat there in stunned silence, until a sharp but quiet voice hissed something unintelligible into his right ear.

"No!" he screamed at the top of his lungs before fleeing from the vehicle.

Andre sprinted through his house and out the front door, running straight through his yard. He continued into the street, where he had no plans of stopping until his mind felt it was safe. Andre sprinted until he was on the main road leading out of his neighborhood. Before he could continue, a series of loud screeches filled his ears, making it almost impossible to move. He cried out in agony as a wave of hopelessness washed over him. It took him several moments due to the screeches, to realize that his legs were carrying him back home against his will. He desperately tried to regain control of his limbs, but he found the effort to be futile.

"Please don't do this," Andre whispered in vain to the invisible forces that drove his movements.

His body didn't listen to him and continued to head back home. Andre couldn't help but weep from the knowledge of what awaited him. He desperately scanned the houses around him for someone who could help, but everywhere he looked, he was met by eyes that were filled with the same despair as him. The screeches eventually faded away but were quickly replaced by dozens of different voices whispering all at once inside his head. All the voices were speaking different things, so his mind was filled with a jumble of incoherent babbling that further fractured his sanity.

By the time he was brought back to his home, Andre had given up all hope of anyone rescuing him. His legs carried him to just a few steps from the door before finally stopping. Andre stood there in shock as he tried to look away from the gateway. He brought his focus towards the sounds of nearby wailing and noticed a husband and wife openly weeping on their lawn directly in front of a door of their own. Andre forced his body to scan the area around him, allowing him to see his neighbors bawling their eyes out before their own hellish gateways. The sounds of wails filled the air and were quickly followed by the noises of doors being pulled open.

Andre gasped in horror as the world around him became filled with the unnatural red color he had been exposed to the night before. Horrifying screams of agony and pain filled his mind, driving him down to his knees. He craned his head to see his next-door neighbor stepping through a gateway, screaming in terror as they did. A sudden pull forced his head to move towards the door before him. Andre tried with all his might to resist it, but he was ultimately brought to heel before the intricately carved designs covering the white door.

The random patterns that covered the unnatural object slowly began to change before Andre's eyes. Carved images took shape and depicted horrible and obscene acts that he hoped didn't exist. He held tightly to the last bits of sanity still sheltered in his mind while the carvings continued to grow more grotesque. After several minutes of terrifying imagery, the door slowly opened on its own. Through a blast of the unnatural, red light, Andre was subjected to visions that were somehow even more horrific than the acts depicted in the carvings on the door.

As he bore witness to the atrocities playing out before him, the last shreds of his sanity finally snapped. He burst into a hysterical fit of laughter upon feeling his mind break free from the burden of his mundane life. Andre stumbled to his feet in front of the hell portal with a feeling of acceptance that grew inside of him. The voices in his mind spurred him forward as he freely moved through the gateway, becoming fully enveloped in the hellish land-scape that awaited. As if sensing his departure, the door immediately slammed shut before disappearing into thin air, leaving nothing behind.

Several months later, in a country halfway across the globe, a farmer sleepily walked out of his house. As he turned to greet the day, he was met with a door that had not been present the night prior. The farmer tentatively approached it with a mix of curiosity and confusion. He cautiously reached a hand towards the freestanding door, but before he could touch it, it swung open. The farmer was treated to an otherworldly shade of red as something moved towards him through the portal.

Andre eagerly came forth to greet his host, while also showing the world that he had changed greatly since en-tering the gateway. His features morphed and twisted, while his body was elongated and fused together to the point where he had stopped being human and had become something else entirely. Andre lifted a sickle-shaped ap-pendage to greet the farmer, cutting off the man's scream with a quick swipe.

Twisted Branches

Frederique pushed through the last thicket of branches and emerged into the clearing where his cabin sat. He let out a deep sigh as he made his way to the small supply shed located around the back of the property. Frederique placed the shovel he had been carrying inside the small shed and gingerly closed the door, making extra sure to lock it. Before entering the secluded cabin, he took a great deal of time to brush off the dried dirt that clung to his clothes as best he could. Though there was still a layer of filth that covered him as he opened his front door, he wasn't too worried about it being spread about.

The first thing he did once inside, was start up a hot shower to wash away any remaining traces of the wood that still clung to his skin. Partway through the rinse, he had to steady himself against the wall as the day had taken more out of him than he had expected. Digging always did that to him, but this time felt like it had drained him more than usual. He supposed that it was just another way to show how he was aging, a fact that Frederique was not keen to be reminded of. Though his body ached, the hot water helped soothe his muscles as it washed over his skin. The feeling was so enjoyable that he spent over half an hour just standing under the shower nozzle.

By the time he dried off, the sun had completely disappeared from the sky, taking any rays of light with it. As he stepped into his kitchen, Frederique couldn't help but stare out into the blackness of the night. Though the moon gave just enough light to make out the surrounding trees, there was still a dimness to it that one couldn't find in the city. There were no added light sources, and thus, it created a completely different feel to which he found himself drawn. The tiny specks of light just made him feel that much more secluded in those woods, which was exactly what he wanted.

He eventually broke himself away from the window to scrounge something up for dinner. It took longer than it should have thanks to his indecisiveness, but he finally whipped out a frozen pizza he had tossed in the freezer over a year prior. His stomach was already growling by the time he placed the unhealthy dinner into the oven, so the thirty-minute wait for it to cook almost seemed like torture to Frederique's body. To make the situation a little bit harder on himself, there was no TV in the cabin, and he had made sure not to take his cell phone with him. So, there was nothing to occupy his mind while the pizza cooked, besides staring out at the faintly illuminated woods that surrounded him.

As he looked out at the same foliage he had seen mere minutes before, something caught his eye. There was a strange shape that he could just barely make out behind a set of trees at the edge of the thicket surrounding his cabin. Despite the shape not moving, and being at a distance where he could not see any of its details, he still found himself drawn to it. He stared at the foreign object, completely engrossed by it. Frederique was so enthralled by the new addition to the trees that he hadn't noticed mere moments before when the timer on the oven went off. It took the full duration of the alarm blaring before he finally snapped from his daze.

In total, it took the isolated man only two or three minutes to pull the pizza from the oven and return to the window while his dinner cooled down, but he was shocked to see that the object looked as though it had grown in size. He spent several more minutes staring at the thing that was slightly hidden by the trees, all the while, still trying to identify what it could be. Eventually, Frederique brought his attention to the pizza, which had already cooled to room temperature by the time he took his first bite. He grumbled under his breath but made no effort to reheat his meal. Instead, he returned to the window for a third time, still driven to discover what the strange object was.

As he peered out the window once more, he was finally able to make out what he had been staring at for well over half an hour: a gnarly-looking tree. He couldn't help but let out a gasp as the dying plant that he had been observing had somehow managed to make its way to the front of the thicket without him noticing. Now that the object had broken through the clearing, Frederique felt a queasy sensation bubble inside his gut. He scanned the twisted and gnarled branches of the foreign tree that had somehow managed to push itself over two dozen feet in a matter of minutes, a feat that should have been impossible.

Frederique thoroughly scanned the rotted, black bark of the emaciated tree with disgust. The bit of wasting foliage looked as though it shouldn't have been standing, let alone pushing itself through the woods without the use of legs. He knew he should have been more frightened by the anomaly, but the feeble look of the tree made him feel as though he should simply write the whole thing off. The complete absence of leaves or any other foliage only confirmed, in his mind, that he had nothing to fear.

"It's nothing. I'm tired is all. I must have just been spacing out and didn't notice it at first," Frederique chuckled. "The digging must've really worn me out."

With his mind convinced that the sickly-looking tree had always been that close to his cabin, he quickly snarfed down his pizza before shuffling off to bed for the night. As he soundly slept, unbeknownst to him, a change was occurring to the deathly-looking tree just outside his cabin. Several hours later, at the point of the night when his sleep was deep enough that he had started to create dreams, a horrific shriek filled the air. The terrifying cry easily ripped Frederique from his slumber and caused him to break out in a cold sweat. He desperately hoped the shriek had come from his dream, and he tried to convince himself of that. It took a second ear-piercing cry for him to finally, and fearfully, admit that there was something outside the cabin.

Faced with no other option, he slowly got out of his bed, standing on legs that couldn't help but tremble. He tentatively pushed down the sole hallway of the cabin in pitch darkness, far too afraid to turn on any lights. Each blind step only further added to the building terror in Frederique's gut, as his only guide was that of his left hand sliding along the nearest wall. The cabin was almost completely silent, except for the sound of his feet cautiously stepping over the wooden floorboards. For him, the silence was far worse than the sound of the shrieks. At least when the screams filled the air, he could tell where the source of the noise was; without them, he was just a terrified man left alone in the dark.

Despite the overwhelming urge to run back to the bedroom and hide under his covers, he pushed himself down the hallway. When he eventually did exit the hall and enter the living room, the small slivers of moonlight that showed through the cracks in the curtains were a welcome sight for Frederique. There was just enough illumination for him to make his way through the open room without the need for something to guide him along. He paused at the precipice of the living room, where it bled into the kitchen, and realized that he hadn't heard an inhuman scream since leaving his bed. The idea that the shrieks had just been a part of a bad dream, once again, flashed through his mind for a split second before the loud crash of shattering glass brought his full attention to the kitchen.

Frederique's heart raced as he took in quick and shallow breaths. He forced his feet to inch forward, moving further into the kitchen. His eyes easily spotted the dozens of pieces of shattered glass, thanks to the moon's soft illumination. It was clear that something had been at the kitchen window, and this realization only left a single question lingering in his mind. *Was whatever had broken the window still there?* He knew there was only one way to find out, and he took a few seconds to mentally prepare himself for what needed to be done.

Frederique took in several, quick gasps while his adrenaline kicked in. He tensed his leg muscles for a brief moment before scrambling forward to be in a direct line with the broken, kitchen window. Before his feet had even stopped moving, Frederique's gaze was already firmly fixed on the newly formed opening. He was met, to his confusion, with the sight of some unnaturally colored object blocking any chance he had of seeing any further outside his cabin. His fear quickly became mingled with an overwhelming sense of confusion as he came to a sudden stop, carefully placing his feet so as not to step on any glass. The strange anomaly blocking his window seemed as though it was made of bark, but the color of it was much lighter than that of the typical tree that inhabited the woods.

Frederique found his natural curiosity starting to well up, but the terror he felt for whatever had made the shrieking noises still held control of his actions. He stood there in silence for a long time, simply staring at the weird thing that blocked his normally scenic view. Eventually, he managed to build up the courage to tentatively move closer to the broken window. Once he was close enough, he carefully reached out his hand and lightly brushed the tips of his fingers against the surface of the blockage. Sure enough, the gnarled and rough texture was that of any ordinary tree bark, but the color continued to perplex him. Since he was closer, he was able to make out the very light hues and different shades that mixed to create the color of the bark. All those different things combined, made for a color that was not treelike in nature, but yet, was still familiar to him.

It took several, long moments for the realization to hit him of why the color looked so recognizable. Just to confirm the thought, and make sure he wasn't going crazy, he brought his arm up and placed it flat against the bark. As his eyes moved between his appendage and the bark, frantically comparing them, the confirmation of what he had suspected hit him right in the gut. Before he could even fully process the new development, the flesh-colored bark pulled back from the window. Frederique whipped his arm back in a kneejerk reaction, while the thing the bark was connected to moved further back.

In just a few seconds, he was able to see that the object that had been blocking the window was the shriveled

tree from earlier, except that now, the tree wasn't so feeble looking anymore. Its trunk had expanded in width,
while leaves had sprouted out of all the branches, adding a
blood-red color to the already strange palette of the plant.
The gnarled and twisted bits that were there before remained, but even those parts had expanded into something more monstrous. Frederique stood completely still,
frozen in place by the shock of witnessing a tree freely
move. He just stared as the greatly expanded plant slowly
turned itself about.

Frederique quickly got the feeling that the tree was
turning with purpose, as though it wanted to show him
something. Regardless of whether he actually wanted to
see it or not, his feet stayed firmly planted right where
they were, making sure he had no choice but to watch. As
the opposite side of the tree began to come into view, he
noticed a growth that was far larger than the other knots
that dotted the plant's bark. A sensation of dread slammed
into his gut as more of the strange growth became visible to
him. He quickly absorbed the details of the large anomaly
in the bark, noticing lines and curves that should not have
naturally been a part of any tree.

Finally, the anomaly had almost completely made its
way into his line of sight, and he let out a gasp of horror
as he was met by the likeness of a woman's face. It was

as though an artist had perfectly sculpted the image of someone out of bark and attached it to the tree. The plant didn't stop moving there; it continued its long turnabout, revealing more faces as it went. Frederique recognized each of the growths, and in turn, the horrific feeling in his gut intensified. Eventually, the tree did come to a stop, revealing one last face that was embedded in its bark.

Frederique stared at the final face visage a few moments before weakly whispering, "Marisol."

As soon as the name left his lips, the bark eyelids of the growth shot open to reveal a set of human eyes. The same shriek that had pulled Frederique from his sleep ripped forth from the lips of the embedded face. That image alone was enough to send a painful jolt of terror through him, finally kicking his body into gear. He immediately turned and scrambled away from the window. As he did so, a giant tree branch punched itself through the broken glass. By sheer, dumb luck alone, he managed to avoid being demolished by the branch as it shot past him.

Without taking a second to think, he sprinted for the front door of the cabin. He immediately flung it open and raced outside, not even bothering to put on shoes. Frederique bounded into a thicket of trees as the abomination continued to roar in anger. As he moved through the forest, he found himself being slowed by an abnormally large number of branches. There were hundreds of them, bunched together into a dense thicket that he found nearly impossible to push through. If a massive surge of adrenaline hadn't been flowing through his veins, he knew he would have surely been brought to a dead halt.

Another horrific shriek penetrated through the air, and he felt a jolt pushing him faster through the thicket. He slashed out at the branches with the full might of his arms, desperately trying to knock them out of the way. Though he was progressing, the shrieks continued and seemed to be drawing closer. Frederique frantically scrambled forward with every ounce of energy he had. Finally, his arms felt out in front of him and found what seemed like the end of the thicket. A small bit of hope filled him and he lunged forward through the last, dense grouping of branches.

Frederique's full weight easily pushed him out of the thicket and into a clearing. He stumbled for a few awkward strides before tripping over into the dirt. Several coughs immediately escaped from his throat, thanks to the particles of dirt he had accidentally inhaled during the fall. After his airway was once again properly working, he pulled himself to his feet and scanned the area for where to go next. As his gaze moved over the clearing, he immediately realized where he was. Frederique looked a few feet in front of him to spy a bit of freshly dug earth, something he had done less than 24 hours prior.

Suddenly, he felt something grab hold of his left ankle. Before he could comprehend what was happening, he was forcefully yanked into the air. Frederique frantically tried to reach for his gripped appendage to pull himself free of whatever was holding him, but it was ultimately futile. A few seconds later, he was slammed into the ground with such tremendous force that the air was completely knocked free from his lungs. He had no time to recover before he was hoisted into the air again. His body slightly turned as it hung in the air, and he caught a glimpse of the monstrous tree out of the corner of his eye. Just as he realized that it was one of the abomination's vines that had grabbed ahold of him, he was slammed against the ground again.

For the second fall, Frederique landed on his right side, with most of his weight pressing against his leg. A split second after he had slammed against the ground, he heard a snapping sound as a burst of agony flew up his right leg. He couldn't help but let out a wail at the top of his lungs as he desperately grasped for the injured appendage. The tree limb that had been wrapped around his left ankle slowly loosened itself, to his surprise. Frederique gently cradled his broken leg with his hands as the tree's onslaught ceased for a moment. This did not last long, however, for only a minute passed before a tree limb shot forward and wrapped itself around his left thigh.

"What are you doing!" he cried out. "Don't!"

The branch began to tighten, applying a great deal of pressure. Frederique felt a new pain radiate through his non-broken leg as it became all too apparent what the tree was going to do. He tried to rip himself free of the monstrosity's grasp, but the pain was so immense that he couldn't even flail his arms. The pressure continued to build as the branch squeezed ever tighter, bringing more screams of agony forth from his lips. Finally, a loud crack sounded as his left leg was broken.

Now that both of his legs had been rendered useless, he could see that there was no way he would outrun the horrible thing he sat before. Tears of pain and despair streaked down his face as he uncontrollably bawled. The tree gave him no sympathy, wrapping a branch around Frederique's right ankle and hoisting him into the air. Frederique managed to let out a quick cry of terror before he was thrown back towards the ground. He closed his eyes as he braced for an impact that came only moments later. Several unspeakable waves of pain traveled up his body from his lower torso thanks to the fact that he, once again, landed in a way where his legs absorbed most of the impact.

Frederique let out wails of agony for several long minutes as the pain kept him completely immobile. His mind was solely focused on the pain, so he gave no thought to what the tree was doing while he was screaming his lungs out. Eventually, the pain subsided enough for him to crack open his eyes. Frederique gasped in utter horror as he found that he had been tossed into a freshly dug hole that was roughly six feet deep. He brought his gaze up to the top of the hole to see all eleven women's faces attached to the tree staring down at him. Each one's gaze was filled with absolute hatred for him.

"I-I-I'm sorry," he whimpered, "I didn't mean to do it. It's a disease. I can't help myself." Frederique desperately pleaded, "I'll never do it again. I promise."

A loud scraping sound came from overhead as the tree pushed a large clump of dirt into the hole. Frederique cried out in fear as the soil fell onto him, beginning the process of enveloping his body. There was but a moment's pause before the next grouping of dirt was pushed into the hole, which was a large enough amount to completely cover his broken legs. He continued to beg for mercy as soil rained down upon him. After only a few minutes, Frederique's body was all but covered by the dry soil, leaving only his head exposed.

"P-Please just let me go," Frederique whimpered.

All eleven faces on the tree responded to his pleas by letting out an inhuman cackling in unison. Another swath of dirt was pushed into the hole, completely covering his head, officially burying him alongside his victims.

Catastrophic Holiday

Sampson glanced around the table at his family and couldn't help but smile. For all the craziness that had come with the year, it was almost unreal how everyone still managed to come together. Sampson had never realized how hard it was to play host for Christmas, but the past few days had quickly shown him. The in-laws had been staying with them, and that in itself was enough to drive Sampson mad. Add on that several of his aunts and uncles had also decided to say they were coming at the last minute, and the whole thing was a logistics nightmare. Yet, despite all the things working against them, he and Michelle had managed to pull it off.

He glanced at his beautiful wife sitting at the other end of the table and smiled at her. She smiled in turn before taking a quick bite of green bean casserole. Sampson nodded to himself while having another look around the large table at all the family members eating and enjoying themselves. He finally stabbed a bit of turkey and brought it up to his lips. The turkey was his favorite part of the holidays, and seeing as most of the family were ham people, it looked like he was going to get a lot of leftovers. As he savored the taste of the dark meat in his mouth, the family dog walked over to the window directly to the right of the table and started barking.

"What's wrong, boy?" Sampson's son, Tony asked.

Sampson took another bite of turkey as he tried to ignore the dog, but Einstein continued to bark with growing fury. Finally, Sampson shouted, "Einstein! Stop barking! You dumb dog, the one time you aren't licking your nuts and it's to ruin our dinner."

Normally, yelling at Einstein was enough to get him to stop. So, when his dog continued to bark, he realized that there was something or someone outside. Just as he was about to get up from his seat to investigate, a large object came crashing through the window, sending shards of broken glass through the air. Sampson's father-in-law happened to be sitting in the direct path of the shards, and his back was immediately peppered with several medium-sized pieces of glass. Shrieks of surprise filled the room as Michelle's father let out a labored gasp before falling onto the table while blood poured from his mouth.

Sampson brought his gaze toward the window to find out what had broken through and discovered the culprit standing mere feet from the table. A creature that must have been nearly six feet in height was looking over the cast of his family, seemingly sizing them up. The beast had black fur and its ears resembled that of a large feline. He would have believed it was just a big cat, except it was standing on two legs. Besides its fur and several other catlike features, the thing had a body type that resembled a human.

"What the hell are you?" Uncle Rico shouted.

The creature must not have appreciated the yelling, as it let out a hiss that was exactly like something a cat would do if it felt threatened. Before anyone could react, the beast leapt over the table and onto Uncle Rico. The abomination's claws tore into Rico, and giant gashes immediately began to form in his flesh. Everyone at the table flew from their seats, fleeing in absolute terror while Sampson sat there in shock as he watched the beast continue to rip chunks of meat from Uncle Rico. His relative weakly reached out a hand toward him just as the beast sunk its teeth into the doomed man's neck. Sampson gasped in disgust as the thing pulled its head back, sending blood and pieces of flesh spilling from Rico's neck.

"Jesus Christ!" he gasped as he stumbled to his feet.

The cat creature suddenly turned and growled at him, sending a feeling of dread through his body. Sampson desperately tried to decide what to do, but his mind wasn't working as the beast took a few steps toward him. He knew that he was about to be ripped to shreds by the monster, but then a yellow flash slammed into the beast. It took a few seconds for him to realize that Einstein had thrown himself at the thing to protect him. Seizing the moment, while his dog kept the creature distracted, he rushed out of the dining room in search of his wife and son.

As he raced into the living room, Sampson noticed that the front door was wide open. After taking a few steps toward it, he realized that the bodies of his great aunt and uncle were lying on the floor. Blood covered the hardwood underneath the two corpses, and he knew the bodies were a warning to let him know he shouldn't try to go outside. He took a few steps toward the carcasses and got a good look at how mutilated they were. One glance at the decimated left eye socket of his great aunt, and he almost puked right then and there. He quickly turned from the carnage and looked toward the stairs.

The thought of hiding in his bedroom had briefly passed through his mind, but one glance up the steps told him that wasn't a good idea. Another one of the cat creatures, this one having orange fur, watched him from the top step. He took a deep breath as the beast simply stared at him. Sampson quickly ran through his options and realized he hadn't tried the basement yet. The monstrosity took a gentle step down the stairs, and he took off. He heard the creature hiss and knew it was coming after him. Sampson sprinted the dozen or so feet to the door that led to the basement and frantically tried to open it. Despite his better judgment, he looked over his shoulder to see that the monster had made it to the ground floor and was charging toward him.

Desperately, he gave a hard yank and the door flew open, pushing him to the side. The creature leapt through the air, not processing that the door was opened, and flew straight through it. Sampson heard the sound of the beast tumbling down the stairs. He scrambled to the doorway and peered down to see the monster lying on the bottom step, crying out in agony. Sampson quickly shut the door behind him before he made his way down the stairs. Once he was a few steps from the injured beast, he took in a deep breath then leapt forward as far as he could in an attempt to avoid getting too close to the monster.

Thankfully, he managed to clear the stairs and landed on the ground a good three or four feet in front of the creature. He quickly maneuvered further back from the beast and took a moment to catch his breath. A sudden feeling of something touching his shoulder had him spinning around to see Michele with a nervous smile spread across her face. He immediately wrapped his arms around his wife and hugged her tightly.

"You made it," he said in relief.

"Of course," Michelle replied, "I took Tony and immediately hid down here."

Sampson pulled back from Michelle and glanced behind her to see his son standing next to his workbench. He smiled as he looked his wife in the eyes. "I'm so glad you're safe."

The wounded creature on the stairs continued to howl in pain, and the three looked over toward it. They watched as the beast rolled off the last step and onto the ground, but didn't attempt to come at them. Instead, the creature just lay there, howling in agony as it tried to grasp its right leg. Sampson noticed a small bit of bone sticking out of the monster, and he knew that the thing had broken its leg. He made his way over to his workbench and scanned the surface of it before picking up a hammer.

"What are you doing?" Michelle asked.

"Well... I'm gonna take this hammer and then I'm gonna hit that thing with it," Sampson replied with a shrug.

"I don't think it's a good idea to get so close to it," Michelle said.

"It'll be fine," Sampson insisted as he took a step toward the creature. "Would you rather sit here and listen to it cry out in pain?"

"No," Michelle grumbled.

Sampson advanced toward the abomination to where he was standing directly over it. The beast hissed at him and tried to swipe at his legs. He hopped back a step, just narrowly avoiding the creature's claws, and swung the hammer. The tool came down and connected with the beast's right arm, which led to a nice cracking sound. Despite the satisfying noise, he brought the makeshift weapon down a few times on the arm until he was certain he had broken it. From there he swung the tool down onto the creature's head. It took several hits for blood to start spurting out, and a few more for the monster to completely stop moving. Once he felt that the beast was dead, he stepped back from it, letting the hammer drop to the ground.

"It's done," he said turning back toward his family.

"Oh my god, you're covered in blood!" Michele exclaimed.

Sampson glanced down at his Christmas sweater to see that it was now colored crimson. There was enough blood on his garments that they stuck to his skin when he walked. He shook his head then took the bottom of his sweater and wrung it out between his hands. Several small streams of crimson dripped out of the fabric and landed on the floor. Michele gagged at the sight as Tony cringed in disgust.

"Well... I did it," Sampson said as he gestured at the creature. "I killed that thing, and it only cost a perfectly good sweater."

"It's a cat person, Dad," Tony cut in.

"A what?" Sampson asked.

"A cat person," Tony explained. "It's a shapeshifter. A person that can turn into an animal. It just so happens that this one could turn into a cat."

"Alright, then I killed the cat person," Sampson sarcastically clarified.

He approached his workbench again and opened up the bottom drawer. Sampson quickly pulled out a little black box and placed it on the ground. Opening the metal container, he took the gun that was placed in it and quickly loaded it.

"When did you get a gun?" Michelle asked in surprise.

"Uhm... that doesn't matter right now," Sampson said, completely avoiding the question as he stood up and moved toward the stairs. That was an argument that would have to wait until after they dealt with the vicious things occupying their house.

"Wait!" Michelle hissed. "You're not actually going up there, are you?"

Sampson nodded. "I'm not having these disgusting creatures rip apart my family and force us to hide in the basement. This needs to be done."

"Okay," Michelle reluctantly agreed, "but be careful."

"I will," Sampson replied as he carefully made his way up the stairs.

As he approached the door to the basement, he took in a deep breath and then placed an ear against it. He carefully listened for a few seconds without hearing anything. Sampson hoped the lack of noise meant that the cat people had left, but he knew that was probably just wishful thinking. He slowly turned the doorknob and let the door creak open just a little. With a deep breath in, he readied himself before throwing the door open and charging out with his gun raised. He did a quick scan of the space directly in front of him and found that it was empty.

A sudden breaking of glass came from the kitchen and he immediately made his way over to it. He poked his head around the corner to find a cat person with white fur throwing some rather expensive wine glasses from his cabinets. Sampson sprang out from around the corner and opened fire. He let off three shots, two of them hitting the creature directly in the chest while the third missed, putting a nice hole in some drywall. The beast stumbled for a bit before trying to leap toward him. He fired off a fourth shot that happened to hit the monster directly in the head, killing it instantly.

A second after he had taken down one of the cat people, he felt a sudden pain streaking down his back. The sound of fabric ripping filled the air and he stumbled forward while grunting in pain. He spun around to see a second abomination with white fur growling at him. Sampson quickly fired off three shots that peppered the beast's chest and sent it to the ground. The creature cried out in agony as it writhed on the floor. Wanting to conserve some ammunition, he removed a butcher's knife from his cutting block and used that to finish off the beast. It took eight stabs with the blade and a large splattering of blood, but he managed to put an end to the monster.

The sound of something moving in the dining room caught his attention, and he headed that way. He noticed that two cat people were in there; one was the black-furred thing from before, while the other was grey. Sampson checked his ammo count to find he only had four bullets left. Knowing he would have to be efficient with how he did things, he prepared to make his move. He sprang into the dining room and fired off two shots at the grey creature's legs. Both of his shots hit their targets, and the beast fell to the floor.

Seeing its comrade injured, the black-furred monster growled at him in anger. Sampson fired off two more shots just as the beast was starting to move. Only one of the bullets landed, hitting the cat person in the left leg. The shot caused the creature to be off-balanced as it leapt toward him, which was all he needed to sidestep the beast. He noticed the gray monster had started to crawl toward him and he decided to take care of that one first. Sampson ran over to the beast and brought the knife down into the back of the creature's neck. The thing gurgled as blood spurted from its throat, quickly staining the carpet beneath. He gave a quick twist with the knife as his own version of a killing blow before yanking the blade free.

Suddenly, a force slammed into his back and sent him to the ground. The black-furred creature clawed away at his back, ripping his skin apart. Sampson screamed out in agony as he desperately swiped the knife behind his back. The blade barely managed to connect with the creature, but that was enough to get the beast off him. He pushed himself off the ground using his hands, and as he came up, he quickly spun around to deliver a stab that caught the monster right in the gut. The cat person shrieked at him, but he simply held the knife in place. A wave of overwhelming anger surged inside of him, and he pulled the blade out only to drive it back in.

Sampson started to widely stab into the beast's abdomen as he shouted, "You come into my home, kill my family, and ruin my Christmas dinner! But most importantly, you stopped me from eating my turkey! No one and nothing comes between me and my holiday turkey!"

Bringing the knife out for a mere second, Sampson drove it back into the beast one final time. The monster shook for a few moments before falling backward onto the floor as its entrails poked out from its abdomen. He stood there gasping for breath while he watched the creature slowly die. As soon as the life left the beast's eyes, he wandered over to the table and plopped down. He looked at the decimated table and noticed that the turkey still lay on it, almost completely undisturbed. Sampson reached for it and ripped a medium-sized chunk of meat off.

He took a bite out of the chunk as he whispered to himself, "Merry fucking Christmas."

Shadow of the Portmouth Stretch

The unrelenting waves slammed against the ship's side, almost pushing seawater onto the boat. Theron Pinkel felt a little of the liquid splash his face, bringing the taste of salt into his mouth. He stepped back, deciding that he would rather not be sprayed again. A loud laugh in his ear broke his attention away from the sea.

"Not fond of getting splashed, aye Professor?" Strips joked, "Looks like you've still got stumps where your sea legs should be!"

Several other crew members joined in laughing with Strips.

"Are all the lines tied down, Strips?" boomed a voice from above them.

They turned to see Captain LeRoe descending the stairs leading to the wheelhouse. Captain LeRoe was a grizzled man in his mid-fifties who was well above six feet in height. Even for his age, he kept himself in great shape. He was a no-nonsense leader who commanded a great amount of respect from his crew, which was evident every time he gave a command. Even when he was addressing only one member of the crew, all hands snapped to attention.

"Well, Strips? Are the lines all tied down?" LeRoe questioned again.

Strips stuttered for a second, in the same manner a small child does when they have been caught doing something they're not supposed to. The words, "No sir!" fumbled out of the sailor's mouth.

"Well, best get to it!" LeRoe barked.

Theron couldn't help but chuckle to himself as he watched Strips scramble off to the opposite side of the deck.

LeRoe made his way over to him. "Sorry about that, Professor." He gave Theron a light slap on the back, causing him to fall forward a bit.

Even though Theron was not a diminutive man himself, his stature was still dwarfed in comparison to the captain's.

"Oh, it's not a problem," he replied. "I do just want to reiterate that I'm not a professor."

LeRoe chuckled. "We know that, but you'll have to forgive my crew. It's not every day that we have an educated man aboard the ship. I think Flint came up with the name." He gestured towards a man currently helping tie down supplies. "Once he comes up with a nickname, the whole crew is saying it by the end of the day. So, I'm afraid it looks like you're stuck with it."

Theron sighed, accepting the fact that he would have to endure a misleading nickname until their journey was over. He looked out over the endless stretch of sea before them. "How much longer till we reach our destination, Captain?" Theron inquired.

LeRoe scratched the back of his neck. "I would say we've got about another day until we near where your colleagues should be." He looked away from Theron as if he was deliberately trying to avoid his gaze. It was clear there was something LeRoe wanted to say, but couldn't figure out how to bring it up.

Theron's curiosity got the better of him and he asked, "Is something wrong, Captain?"

LeRoe moved his gaze to the sea, still not making eye contact with Theron. "Oh, it's nothing really. An old wives' tale more than anything." He continued to insist, "It's just a bit of superstition."

Theron could see that the captain's words contradicted his body language. Even if it was nothing more than a small superstition, it was clearly upsetting him. He did not want the leader of the ship he was on to be in a distressed state of mind. LeRoe would be much less likely to make a costly mistake with clear thoughts.

"Captain, it seems that whatever is bothering you… it has at least given you some modicum of anxiety. Please, tell me what is on your mind. Even if it is nothing more than a superstition, perhaps saying it out loud will set you at ease," Theron said with a light undertone of urgency in his voice.

LeRoe took a deep breath and looked out towards the sea. He asked, "How much do you know about the area we're sailing to?"

Theron shrugged. "Not much, I'm afraid. Just what I've learned from the research my colleagues and I have been conducting. I know it seems to be the likely resting place of several significant, ancient artifacts."

LeRoe nodded his head, and then asked, "Why were you left behind on the mainland while the rest of your group ventured ahead of you?"

Theron replied, "I'm the only one of my peers who is still working on their master's degree. Everyone else is a doctor or working towards it. They agreed to leave for the expedition since they have more education and experience, and were supposed to come back with initial collections of the area by the week's end." He looked LeRoe directly in the eyes. "As you know, the week's end was almost a fortnight ago. It was understood if they hadn't communicated back to anyone at the university that I was to come looking for them."

LeRoe walked over to the side of the boat, placing his hands on the railing. "Aye, I could see how two weeks might be cause for alarm. But maybe your friends just forgot to send word to you," he suggested.

Theron shook his head. "I've never known Dr. Atendon to be anything less than punctual. Either they got lost on the way there, or something horrible happened to them."

LeRoe looked over his shoulder at Theron; he let out a deep sigh. In a calm voice he said, "Well, at this point I would be leaning towards the latter over the former."

Theron stared at the captain with a stunned look plastered on his face.

LeRoe turned his head slightly, just enough to see Theron out of the corner of his eye. He slowly continued in a grave tone, "You must understand Mr. Pinkel, I don't make this statement lightly." He looked back out at the sea. "The island your friends were sailing for is located in a very treacherous part of the ocean. You see, there's a small, two or three mile bit of ocean that is probably some of the deadliest waters in the world. And it just so happens to surround the island you and your friends were hoping to explore."

LeRoe tightened his grip on the railing before he continued. "They call this area the Portmouth Stretch." He paused, "Now they don't call it that because of the town of Portsmouth. No, that's something entirely on its own." He turned around to face Theron, leaning against the rail with his hands still gripping it tightly. "You see, anyone who has sailed in that area will tell you that the waters change once you reach the stretch. They become far more violent, almost like the sea itself is attacking the vessel. Every sailor who has lived to tell the tale has said the same thing. The water seems to be more violent on the port side of the ship."

Theron began to feel a little anxious as LeRoe spoke. The fact that he or his colleagues did not know of the danger surrounding the island made Theron feel extremely uneasy.

The captain continued, "You see, Professor, those who have seen such fierce waters ram up against the port side of their vessel say it looks like a mouth. That's how they say the stretch got its name." LeRoe studied Theron to see his response to the news he had just delivered. He could tell that the young college student had been shaken by his words.

Theron cleared his throat. "Thank you for informing me of this, Captain."

LeRoe put up a hand to silence Theron. "There's something else." He paused, checking to make sure the men were not close to them, and lowered his voice. "Now I don't believe in any supernatural happenings in this world. My crew, however, cling to a different set of beliefs. Some of them seem to think that the waters are haunted. That the stretch is forever tormented by the souls lost to the sea. The way they talk about it, it seems like they think that the apparitions themselves are the cause of the turbulent waters."

Upon hearing LeRoe speak of ghosts in such a genuine tone, Theron felt a bit of his anxiety disappear. He let out a small, unconfident chuckle. "Captain, there's no such thing as undead sailors haunting the sites of their deaths."

LeRoe shushed him. "I said my men fear the supernatural, not me."

Theron turned to walk elsewhere on deck, shrugging off what LeRoe had told him.

LeRoe grabbed hold of his arm, stopping him from walking forward. He whispered in a harsh tone, "Listen boy, the ghosts may not be real, but those waters truly are dangerous. This ship did not avoid the great war only to be sunk by some college student's ignorance."

The captain released his grip on Theron's arm. He pointed his finger at him as if to scold him and continued, "I agreed to sail you to the island because your university was willing to give me quite a large payment," he took a step closer to Theron, "but I tell you now. I value my crew and my ship more than any amount of money. The second I feel that the trip is too dangerous to make, I will turn us around—" LeRoe moved to where he was mere inches from Theron, "—your friends be damned."

The rest of the day, the crew went about their daily tasks as Theron looked through his extensive notes. He wanted to make sure he was prepared, so as not to waste any time once they reached the island. As the night came and Theron lay awake in his bed, LeRoe's words echoed in his mind. The captain did not seem like someone who was shaken by many things. So, the fact that he had lashed out at Theron for his comment bothered him. Theron only hoped that LeRoe would keep himself composed enough for them to safely reach the island. His mind still pondered this as he slowly fell asleep.

Theron awoke to the sound of the men scurrying about the deck. Their feet stomped above where he lay in the sleeping quarters. He felt that the ship seemed to be rocking in a more violent manner than usual, which sent a small wave of panic through him. Quickly, Theron got dressed and made his way onto the deck. He noticed the looks of anxiety on most of the crew's faces, just before a large wave hit the side of the boat, spraying water onto the deck. It was clear that the sea had become more tumultuous overnight. The deck was now covered in seawater that had been tossed onboard by the waves. Theron could easily see it collecting into large masses with the rocking of the ship, no doubt adding to an already escalating problem.

He took a few steps out, hearing the sound of LeRoe dictating orders from above him. He turned to see the captain yelling at his men from just in front of the wheelhouse near the top of the stairs.

Theron jogged up the stairs to LeRoe. "What on earth is happening?"

LeRoe stopped barking orders long enough to answer, "We're getting close to the stretch, Professor. We could enter it at any moment, and I wouldn't say we're prepared for that."

"Is there anything I can do to help?"

The captain looked at him for a moment, as though he was going to turn down the offer. "Go and help Jasper and the others secure our equipment!" LeRoe finally yelled over the crashing waves.

The college student made his way over to the port side of the deck, close to the front of the ship. He could barely hear anything over the pounding of the waves. Theron now noticed that the wind was blowing fiercely, whipping seawater onto his face. He yelled out at Jasper, "The captain sent me to help you get things secured!"

The sailor gave him a nod and handed him a rope. Jasper pointed to the railing. "Wrap the rope around that and make sure it's taut! I'll be right behind you to secure it."

Theron grabbed the rope in his hands, and then slowly began to walk forward. He found it difficult not to fall on the slippery floor of the deck. With a final cautious step, he made it to the railing. Quickly, he wrapped the rope around the railing several times. Theron grabbed hold of the end, pulling back towards him. He used all his might to pull it tight.

"I've got it!"

Jasper moved towards him and reached out to grab the rope, but at that moment a giant wave rocketed over the port side of the boat, almost exactly where Theron and Jasper were standing. Theron felt the overwhelming crush of the large mass of water as it washed over him. He held on to the rope with every bit of strength he had in his body. In a split second, the wave moved over Theron, and he found himself completely soaked. Theron fell to his knees, still barely clutching the rope. He turned, expecting to see Jasper beside him, but found that he was gone.

"Jesus Christ, that was enormous!" Theron heard Jasper yell. He spotted Jasper making his way from the starboard side of the deck back towards him.

"I've never had a wave that tossed me across the deck!" Jasper shouted.

Theron could easily sense the fear in Jasper's voice. If a seasoned sailor like him was fearful of the waves, what did that mean for Theron?

Jasper gestured for Theron to get up. "Come on, we still need to secure the rope!"

Theron pulled himself up and tightened his grip on the rope once more. Jasper proceeded with his duty of properly tying it down. After a few seconds, it was clear that something was wrong.

Jasper yelled over the wind, "The rope is too wet! I can't get a proper grip on it!"

As soon as Jasper finished saying that, another large wave barreled onto the ship. It slammed into Theron and Jasper, pushing them across the deck. The two men collided with the railing on the other side of the ship. Theron lay there, breathing heavily as seawater continued to fall onto him. He felt a hand grab hold of him, pulling him up.

Theron was greeted with LeRoe suddenly yelling at him, "Stay away from the left side of the ship! We've reached the stretch!"

Jasper shouted back, "But we haven't secured the line, Captain!"

LeRoe called out in a demanding voice. "Don't try it, Jasper! The waves are too big for any man to handle. You'll be swept over the side of the ship and be lost to the sea!"

Jasper nodded his head in agreement, and the three moved back a little from the railing. They watched as another wave even larger than the previous two swept over the equipment, engulfing it in an instant. The boat rocked towards the left side in that moment, and the crew could only watch as the unsecured crates were swept off the deck.

Theron could hear Stripes yelling, "Captain, we have to turn around! We can't survive many more of these waves!"

LeRoe immediately responded, "We can't turn back now! The waves are too big. If we try to turn, the ship will capsize! Our only choice is to hold tight and hope the waves will let up enough that we can weigh anchor close to the island!" LeRoe grabbed hold of Theron's collar.

"It looks like you'll be making it to your island after all, Professor!"

"My god!" screamed Jasper.

They all turned to the port side just in time to see a massive wave towering over the ship. For a second, Theron swore he could see something, almost reminiscent of a mouth in the seismic amount of water. Then the wave hit the boat, knocking all the men off their feet. Theron felt water enter his mouth, choking off his breath, then he was slammed against the deck as the wave rushed over him and spilled off the starboard side of the ship. He turned onto his stomach and coughed up the saltwater, wheezing heavily. Theron looked up to see Stripes leaning over the side, desperately searching the water.

Stripes turned back to the other men and screamed, "Lempke got knocked off the ship! We have to find him!"

LeRoe ran over to Stripes, firmly grabbing hold of his shoulders and starting to shake him. "Lempke is gone, Stripes! There's no use getting lost to the waves yourself in search of him!" LeRoe moved towards the stairs leading to the wheelhouse. "We need to stay away from the edges! Everyone move back towards the wheelhouse!"

Theron felt himself being pushed forward by the other men as they stumbled their way towards the stairs.

"Hold strong, men!" LeRoe shouted. "I promise you we will make it through these waters!"

As if the sea had heard him and took offense to his promise, another wave slammed the port side. The men huddled together, waiting to see if another wave was coming forth. Theron could sense something; the boat's rocking was starting to subside. A few more waves hit the sides of the boat, but they were much less severe than what had come before. Each of the men breathed an audible sigh of relief at the realization the waters were calming down. LeRoe moved past the men, pushing them out of the way. He made his way further out onto the deck, studying the sea in both directions.

"The waves have died down, and the wind along with them."

Theron immediately noticed the slight feel of a breeze barely blowing against his face, which was a much more calming sensation than what he had been subjected to mere minutes prior.

Jasper asked, "Do you know why the waters calmed down, Captain?"

LeRoe pointed towards the front of the vessel. "I don't know for sure, Jasper. All I know is that we're less than a mile from the island."

The men walked towards LeRoe, looking out over the ocean. They were each able to spot the small island, now well within their field of vision.

"There's something coming up on our port side, Captain!" Stripes suddenly shouted.

LeRoe pushed through the men and went over to where Stripes was standing. Looking out, he noticed the shape of a sea-torn ship not that far in front of them. The vessel was no more than half a mile from the island's shore.

"That might be my colleagues' ship!" Theron gasped in shock.

Stripes whispered to LeRoe, "I don't think we should approach it, Captain, something seems off about it."

LeRoe brought his full attention to the ship before them. It didn't look like the vessel had been caught on a sandbar or any large rocks, yet it was just sitting there in the open waters. It was clear that it had been battered by the same waves they had faced, though there didn't seem to be any damage that kept it from sailing the rest of the way to the island. Plus, it looked like the anchor had been dropped, which meant it was free-floating there; that wasn't the part that disturbed LeRoe, though. It was the fact that he didn't see any signs of people on the vessel. No one was on the deck, and there was no visible movement coming from anywhere else on the ship.

Theron could see a look of fear spread across LeRoe's face. He watched as LeRoe began to run across the deck towards the wheelhouse.

"What's wrong, Captain?" Stripes asked as LeRoe pushed past him.

LeRoe grabbed hold of the helm, quickly turning the wheel. He groaned as he started to turn the vessel to the right. "Something happened to that ship!" LeRoe yelled to the crew. "I don't know what, but I know I don't want to find out!"

Theron could feel the boat cut through the water as it shifted in direction. He could see that with their new trajectory, they would sail past the island. Theron called to LeRoe, "Captain! You're going to miss the island!"

"Aye, Professor! I'm going to hook us to the far side of the island, then we'll land. I want to avoid getting near that ship at all costs."

LeRoe held the helm steady, letting the ship even itself out. Theron could see that the captain would easily put a good amount of distance between them and the abandoned ship. Even with the gentle breeze, it seemed that they would be able to reach the island in less than half an hour. The boat gave a sudden lurch to the right, accompanied by a noise that sounded as if it had slammed into something. LeRoe was thrown off balance, almost losing his grip on the steering wheel.

Stripes yelled out in surprise, "Did we hit a rock?"

LeRoe regained his balance, tightening his grip on the wheel. The large stone of fear forming in his gullet made him completely oblivious to Stripes' question.

"Captain!" Theron shouted at LeRoe to break him out of his trance. As the dazed man looked at Theron he asked, "Did we hit a rock?"

LeRoe shook his head while quietly whispering, "No."

Everyone felt another hit land on the bottom left side of the ship. Theron stumbled a few steps, almost falling onto the deck. He looked down to see the floor rushing towards him. Throwing his left hand against the deck for support he managed to stop his fall, though his left knee still slammed against the wood. Theron let out a grunt of pain as he looked up towards the crew members. He saw nothing but looks of pure fear spread across their faces, each one seeming to know something that Theron didn't.

Theron heard Stripes let out a yell of terror at something off to the left side of everyone. He turned towards the source of the crew's panic and a wave of terror ran through him as his eyes witnessed something massive rising far above the ship's deck. A humongous creature suddenly came into view, easily towering over them. Theron surmised that it was at least 100 feet high. The thing seemed to not have any discernable shape, its body being one, smooth form. Theron could swear he was able see through the creature even though the dark color of it should have made such a feat impossible. The thing's color was reminiscent of a shade of black one would see if they looked back at their own shadow. It was as if a large shadow had formed into an actual gigantic mass of sentience.

LeRoe cried out, "Get away from it!"

He shouted to several crew members who had stumbled to the left side of the boat. Theron looked at the men who were frozen in fear at the sight before them, not able to move himself. The creature seemed to respond to LeRoe's shouts by making a loud noise that was akin to a horrifying gurgling sound. Before the men's eyes, a large chunk of the creature seemed to start to rip away from the shapeless blob. The chunk stopped splitting away roughly halfway down the visible part of the creature. The new mass began to stretch out forward over the deck, forming itself into something that resembled an appendage.

Theron realized what the creature was doing just in time to scream, "It's going to hit the deck!"

Several of the men started to move in reaction to Theron's words, but it was too late. The creature slammed its new appendage down onto the deck, landing upon two of the men. Theron noticed that the men were not crushed, but instead, had become enveloped by the appendage. They were still alive, desperately struggling inside of the creature to escape. Theron started to run forward to help, but he felt someone grab ahold of him. He looked over his shoulder to see that LeRoe had moved down onto the deck and was holding him back.

Theron glanced at LeRoe, seeing the solemn look on his face. He was about to protest but then LeRoe shook his head to let him know there was nothing he could do. Theron looked at the two men struggling to claw their way out of their prison. He could see they were in great amounts of pain. Their mouths were opened wide as if to scream, but no sound was coming out. Then, everyone watched in horror as a large patch of skin began to melt off one of the men's faces. Theron let out a cry of horror as the men began to slowly disintegrate, their skin melting away from their bodies.

LeRoe loosened his grip on Theron, letting him stumble a few feet forward. Theron's eyes did not leave the two men. Their melted flesh moved off their bodies and into the creature before slowly being dissolved away. Theron pulled his gaze away as the last of the unfortunate men's bones finally disappeared. The whole horrifying process only took thirty to forty seconds, but to Theron it felt as though it had taken hours. All onboard the vessel were left frozen in absolute terror at what they had just witnessed.

The creature let out another loud, gurgling noise before swiping the appendage across the deck again. Several of the men managed to dive out of the way, but most were caught by the creature. Theron looked to see Stripes had been one of the ones caught; the unfortunate soul silently screamed with tears floating from his eyes into the mass he was encased in. LeRoe grabbed hold of Theron and spun him around.

LeRoe stared Theron dead in the eyes and said, "We have to abandon ship now!"

Theron simply shook his head in agreement as his mind tried to process what was happening.

LeRoe pointed to the right side of the ship. "Make way to the railing and jump over!"

The two men took off at a full sprint for the other side of the ship. Theron grabbed hold of the rail and flung himself over. As he fell, he heard a scream of fear, mixed with another horrific gurgling noise from the creature. Theron hit the water with a forceful thud, which felt like a block of concrete slamming against his back. He felt a wave of pain surge through him, filling him with adrenaline. Theron pushed with all his might, forcing his way to the surface. He broke through the water with rasping gasps, taking in as much air as possible. Theron then called out, "LeRoe! LeRoe!"

He scanned the waters around him for any sign of the captain. Theron wasn't able to see a single trace of him. That's when he realized it was LeRoe's scream he had heard before he plunged into the water. Though completely distraught at the certain death of LeRoe, Theron knew it wouldn't be long before the creature went looking for survivors. Quickly, he began to paddle with all his might toward the island. He swam forward at a less-than-desirable pace, but he was still managing to make sizable progress. After roughly half an hour of furious paddling, he was just a few hundred feet from the island. He heard a loud splintering noise and looked behind him to see the creature decimating the ship. Theron pushed himself even further with each stroke until he finally felt his feet kick at sand beneath him.

He stopped swimming and let his feet touch the ground before he stood and staggered his way out of the water, onto the island before him. Theron was about to fall to his knees when he heard the loud sound of the creature far behind him. He decided it would be best to keep moving, staggering further inland on the island. There was a large growth of plant life placed out before Theron, so he decided to make the most of it and immediately headed for the nearest tree line. He desperately hoped the foliage would conceal his presence from the creature.

Theron pushed forward through the thicket, making his way further inland, his exhaustion greatly slowing down any progress. After several minutes of staggering, he collapsed against a nearby tree. He sunk onto his knees, breathing heavily. Theron looked around as he let out long winded breaths. He leaned his back up against the tree, while his eyelids began to drop as he fought to keep them open. The inevitable came and Theron slowly drifted off into sleep.

Theron eventually awoke to the sound of something banging in front of him. He scrambled to his feet quickly and began to move in the direction of the noise. Within a few minutes, he was able to spot a clearing ahead of him. As he grew closer, Theron saw movement through the trees, and he realized that someone was there. He slowed down his pace dramatically in an effort to decrease the sound he was making.

Moving with more caution he crept forward, keeping low to the ground. Theron carefully peered out from his hiding spot to get a better look at whoever was making the noise. He saw a young man swinging a machete into a rather large piece of wood. Theron felt a sense of familiarity regarding the man before him. He moved his way around through the foliage to get a better view of the man's face. After a few quick steps, he managed to catch a small glimpse of the stranger's visage. *By god*, he thought, *that's Cory Redford.* He let out a sigh of relief at the discovery that one of his colleagues had survived an encounter with that horrifying creature.

Theron carefully moved out of the brush, walking slowly into the clearing. He cleared his throat before simply saying, "Cory."

The cutting paused as Cory glanced up from the large piece of wood he was working on. His gaze met with Theron's, to which Theron gave a small smile. A look of pure terror crossed over Cory's face as the machete slipped from his hands. It fell, hitting the ground with a loud clang.

Theron took a step closer, "It's me, Cory. It's Theron Pinkel."

Cory let out a scream of panic and turned to run away. He tripped on a root and fell to the ground, quickly turning over to see Theron walking slowly towards him. His colleague scrambled backward, pushing himself back with his hands.

"What's wrong with you, Cory?" asked Theron. "I'm here to help you." Theron held out his hand but it was slapped away.

Cory yelled at him, "You haven't helped me, you've killed me!"

Theron took a step back, slightly fearful of what Cory would do in his current state.

Cory shouted again at Theron, "You saw it, didn't you? You saw that thing!"

Theron nodded, "Yes... yes, I did. What is it?"

Cory let out a fearful laugh. "'What is it?' As if anyone could ever know what that thing is."

Theron took a step towards his comrade and Cory quickly pointed at him.

Cory said in a fearful tone, "It is an ancient creature. A byproduct of Nyarlathotep himself. A thing that has lived in the ocean's deep for many years. It calls this stretch of water its home, while thousands of men have only known it as their grave. A place where it lures unsuspecting fools to their deaths."

Theron looked at his colleague with pity at the state he was in. He asked with a calm voice, "How do you know that it's intelligent enough to trick people into coming here?"

Cory burst into tears; his weeping was almost as loud as his yells from before. He managed to sputter out in between gasps, "I know these things because the last person told them to me."

Theron was puzzled by Cory's last statement. He asked, "What do you mean, the last person?"

Cory brought his head up looking directly into Theron's eyes. He whispered through tears to Theron, "The best way to lure anything is with bait."

The realization hit Theron in an instant. A feeling of terror and guilt filled him. Theron had hired a large crew of men to sail out here to find his colleagues. Unbeknownst to him, it was all according to the plan of an ancient evil. Those poor souls had now been taken as food by that abominable creature, and it was all Theron's fault. He had played right into the hands of an ancient evil. He had doomed at least a dozen men to one of the most horrible deaths imaginable.

Theron looked down at Cory, tears beginning to fill his own eyes. He asked, "What happens now?"

Suddenly, a loud, gurgling noise from beneath them sounded before Cory could speak. He let out a scream of panic just before an explosion came from the ground. A massive part of the creature burst forth, enveloping Cory. Theron stared in horror as he watched his peer slowly disintegrate away within the creature. He could only imagine Cory's pained screams as the flesh melted away from his bones. Theron didn't look away this time. He watched the whole process.

As soon as the last bit of Cory dissolved, the creature disappeared back into the earth, leaving Theron there in stunned disbelief. Theron realized why he had been able to survive an encounter with the creature. He was the bait now. Theron was now nothing more than a piece of bait that would lure more unfortunate souls to the island to be consumed by the evil that lurked in the ocean's depths. Nothing would be able to stop it from claiming the next group of victims. Theron only had one hope that lingered in his mind now. He hoped that no one would come looking for him.

The Same Earth as His Father

GERMAIN CAME TO A sudden stop as he spied the tiniest movement in the gravel floor of the subbasement. There was no way he was taking a chance by staying to see what exactly was happening, so he immediately turned to head up the stairs. As he scrambled up the wooden steps he had installed years ago, he could just barely make out the sound of dirt sifting about. Despite all his instincts to keep moving, Germain took a quick peek over his shoulder to witness layers of dirt swirling around, morphing together to create something new.

The feeling of terror that had plagued him for many nights in the past welled up inside, reaching a level far greater than anything he had ever felt before. Germain's legs carried him up the stairs with a tremendous speed that he never knew he possessed. The moment he emerged into the manmade basement of his home, he immediately slammed shut the steel door leading to the sublevel. He fumbled for a moment to close the padlock before securing the other locks on the door.

After he had finished closing the barrier between him and the anomaly below, Germain was left with a brief moment of respite from the terror. Part of him truly believed that the concrete basement would be enough to stop it, but he knew that wasn't true. If a layer of concrete was all it took to stop the curse that had been levied against his family, then his father would still be alive and well. Instead, his dad had been taken by the earth itself and was probably buried somewhere in the very soil that had enveloped his grandfather so many years ago. Now it was coming for him, just like it had with his father, and his grandfather, as well as dozens of generations of the Holtzclaw family.

A sudden banging against the metal door startled him and he began to run for the stairs. Germain started to climb, but stopped on the third step as the banging continued. There was something about the sound that told him the thing could not break through his barrier. He allowed himself to exhale a light sigh of relief, thinking to himself that perhaps all the time and labor he had placed into the significant layer of protection were finally paying off. A few more bangs sounded off before abruptly stopping, leaving his heavy breathing as the only noise in the basement.

Germain took a very tentative step down the steps, driven by a curious desire that he knew he probably shouldn't heed. Regardless of what his instincts told him, he proceeded back to the basement floor and began to cautiously approach the metal door. The silence that hung in the air signaled to him that it was okay to continue onward. Once he had reached the metal barrier, Germain pressed his ear up against its cold surface. He intently listened, expecting to hear some noise coming from the other side of the door, but none came. Eventually, he slowly backed away, satisfied that he had kept the earth at bay for the night.

As he crossed back to the stairs, a split second of movement caught his eye. He turned to find the tiniest specks of dirt whirling about on the concrete floor. Even with all the precautions he had taken, Germain forgot one simple thing, and that was that concrete came from the earth. It was made up of many things of course, but dirt was one of them.

Though it was nearly impenetrable, there must have been chunks of the concrete floor that were loose enough for the earth to mold and shape. A horrible sinking feeling fired itself into his gut and he immediately sprinted to the stairs.

There was no time to waste, and he flew to the top of the steps in a matter of seconds. He only glanced down the stairs for a moment, and that was all he needed to see the swirling dust had significantly grown in size. At the pace the earth was invading his basement, Germain calculated he had but a few minutes until it came for him once more. That was something he hoped to prevent as he switched on the water attachment placed on the sturdy wall leading down into the basement. He gave it a few moments for the water to start properly flowing before frantically throwing open the door of the metal cabinet attached to the wall and pulling the firehose from it.

Germain unreeled the hose, feeding the long object down the steps with precision in each and every one of his movements. He braced himself against the steps before finally releasing the water and allowing the hose to blast the liquid at full force. Gallons of water spat out of the large nozzle and washed down the steps in a matter of seconds. The force of the blast had him dropping the hose onto the steps and simply allowing the intense water pressure to hold it in place. He eagerly watched as the liquid sprayed downward onto the basement floor, slowly spreading itself out over the concrete.

The swirling twister of dust had grown by a decent amount and was starting to take on the size of a small cloud, but as soon as it came into contact with the water, it sputtered for a moment. Particles of the dust became drenched by the water, which dragged them down to the floor. The continuing stream of liquid swept up the wet particles of earth, and the swirling cloud began to lose some of its mass. Germain allowed himself to feel a small sense of relief as he witnessed his maneuver working. Though he was not completely certain the water would stop the earth in its tracks, he was positive that it bought him a decent amount of time.

Not wishing to tempt fate, he sprinted up the next set of stairs to the top floor of his house. He proceeded with quick and decisive action; each movement he made was filled with deliberate purpose. Germain burst into his bedroom and pulled a suitcase stuffed with packed clothes out from under his bed in one fluid motion. He crossed to the bathroom where a small toiletry bag was plucked from a drawer before being placed in the travel bag. The last thing he took from the room was a sack containing his passport, as well as several large amounts of cash in an array of different currencies.

Germain wasted no time hurrying back down to the ground level of his home, where he immediately headed for the garage. Placing all his packed belongings into the trunk of the hybrid vehicle, he was all but ready to go. However, a small part of him couldn't leave just yet, at least not until he checked on the swirling mass of earth. His instincts screamed at him to simply drive away, but his curiosity, the need to know if the entity was truly incapacitated for the time being, sent him back inside his residence.

The moment he set foot inside his house once more, something about it felt different to him. He couldn't put his finger on what it was, but the atmosphere in his residence felt off to him. This unfamiliar sensation filled Germain with a combination of anxiety and doubt, which added to his trepidation as he slowly progressed across the ground floor. The sounds of gushing water were still prevalent as he carefully proceeded toward the stairs to the basement.

As he drew near, his mind returned to past memories. First, he reminisced on the long hours of preparation and work he had put into crafting the necessary traps to keep the entity from reaching him. Then, his mind turned to the last moments he had shared with his father, as well as the last words spoken from his patriarch's lips.

"It's not after you, Germain," his father had gasped. "Not yet."

The earth itself had surged forth, wrapping itself around his father with unparalleled speed. Germain had only been able to watch as the swirling mass of dirt and soil slowly squeezed the life from his dad. He distinctly remembered the desperate wheezes that were nothing more than futile attempts from his father to breathe in air, while at the same time it was being forcibly expelled from his lungs. The moment that stuck with Germain most of all, the single image that scarred him from that day forth, was seeing one of his father's eyeballs pop out of its socket in tandem with the old man screaming in agony. That sight had driven his actions ever since. Every bit of paranoia, each extra step of precaution had been because of that moment.

A single moment had influenced every decision in his life and had inadvertently placed him at the top of the staircase, staring down into a basement that was quickly starting to flood. Germain had never experienced love or been close to anyone. He had never fully lived out his childhood or the joys of carefree traveling. Instead, he had spent his whole life looking over his shoulder, always wondering if any given day would be his last. He constantly dreaded when the entity crafted of the earth itself would come for him, and it had finally done so.

Germain had been ready for the earth, and that was an accomplishment he could take pride in. However, he felt an entirely different emotion as he stared down the steps at the dense clump of mud that fought against the incredible amount of water spewing forth from the hose. Even with all the liquid being brought against it, the entity had not ceased its pursuit. In fact, the earth had clumped itself together, creating a form that was completely different from what he had witnessed the night his father died. Even more terrifying, it was clear to him that its mass had increased significantly, to the point where it was almost as large as a grown man, and it continued to gain size.

The sight of the growing monstrosity slowly progressing toward him filled Germain with enough dread that he stood frozen in place for several crucial seconds. A final moment or two was all the mass of earth needed to break free of the crushing spray of water and it surged toward him unabated. Germain was able to pull himself from his terror-induced trance and sprinted for the garage, but he was not able to make it far. Something wrapped itself around his left leg as he approached the living room, and he fell to the floor. His body smacked against the hardwood, stunning him in the process. After recovering from the fall, he instinctively flipped onto his back to find that the ever-growing mass of earth was nearly on top of him.

"No!" Germain screamed. "I beat you! This can't be happening!"

The mass of earth ignored his shouts and flung itself onto his legs. In a fluid motion, the wet mud spread out over the rest of his body until coming to a stop just below the neck. The entity pushed down against his body, and he felt an insane amount of force keeping him from moving. He desperately tried to break free, but the strength of the entity was far too much for him to overcome. Germain prepared for the earth to squeeze the life from him, but that didn't happen. Instead, a huge clump of mud moved up his throat, over his chin, and forced its way into his mouth.

Germain gagged at the taste of dirt inside his mouth, but soon the sentient piece of mud forced its way down his esophagus. Before he could properly recover, another patch of mud shoved its way down his throat and into his gut. Dozens of pounds of mud jammed their way inside his body in a matter of minutes, pushing against his entrails until his stomach ripped open. Even after destroying his gut, the mud continued to force its way into him, until it had stretched his skin to the point where it ripped open. Germain ceased moving in that moment and the mud stopped trying to force itself into him, instead beginning the process of moving its victim. Now that its task was complete, the entity was taking him back to where he belonged, the earth. The same bit of earth it had placed Germain's father in all those years prior.

Bleeding Gold

AUSTIN FLUNG OPEN THE door to the bathroom and stumbled over to the nearest stall. After closing the stall door, he frantically fumbled with the lock before finally securing it. He threw down the toilet lid so as not to sit on the disgusting seat that seemed to be covered in feces and crusty puddles of dried urine. Austin violently scratched his legs as he plopped down on the filthy, porcelain throne. He wasted no time in dropping his pants and feeling along his left thigh for several moments before sensing a lump with his fingertips.

Wasting no time, Austin awkwardly reached into his pant pocket, now down by his ankles, and fished out the box of razorblades he had stowed away in it. He took one of the pristine blades from the box and carefully lowered it to just above the spot on his leg where he had felt the lump. Austin took in a deep breath while a mix of anxiety and anticipation made him pause for a moment. Suddenly, a wave of unbearable pain forced Austin's hand, and he slid the blade an inch or two across his left leg, immediately drawing blood. He stared at the crimson liquid for several seconds before a surge of worry slammed into him as Austin noticed the blood looked completely normal.

"Oh god," he whispered to himself in a shaky voice, "I missed the spot."

Austin was a second away from frantically throwing toilet paper onto the wound to stop the bleeding when, to his relief, a hardened speck of yellow crept out of the wound along with the blood. Several more specks quickly followed the first, each growing larger than the last. Austin sucked in a deep breath, then slowly let it out as a feeling of euphoria overtook the horrific pain he had just felt less than a minute ago. His limbs began to relax, and Austin simply stared at the chunks of gold freely flowing from the cut he had just made.

It had been eight months since Austin first got the condition he was currently afflicted with, and the disease seemed to be getting more aggressive by the day. The old bag who put the curse on him must have been incredibly well practiced in the dark arts, because Austin could find no other way to slow down the spread of gold throughout his body. No other way to stop the terrible burning that accompanied the process of his blood slowly turning into a metallic solid. He had to cut his flesh whenever the stinging sensation reared up, or he would be left with a useless body part, like what had occurred to his right pinky.

Austin held the worthless finger up to the light as the euphoria from the cut began to wear off. The small appendage was a sickly yellow color and had permanently hardened to the point where Austin would have to work on it with a pair of sheers for several minutes if he wanted to remove the pinky. It was a preview of the horrifying fate that eventually awaited Austin, no matter how many times he ripped the affliction from his flesh. He glanced back at the cut to see the gold had finally started to clot the open wound, leaving behind a colorful scab that easily stood out against the pale tone of his skin. Austin took a moment to glance over all the other gold-colored scabs that covered his legs, altogether taking up a great deal of his skin's surface area.

He was quickly running out of undamaged patches of skin, which was obviously a huge problem, but there was an even bigger one he had to contend with. Simply put, every time he cut open the part of his flesh that was being attacked by the curse, it felt good. Perhaps too good. It started to seem like nothing else in the world mattered to Austin except for the incredible sensation that overtook him each time he physically cut gold from his body. To make the situation worse, the feeling only managed to last for a minute or two, not nearly enough time to offset the agony endured beforehand.

So, Austin had started to actually want the curse to hit him harder. Sure, that would mean more pain, but it also meant more of that incredible sensation and Austin was fine with that. The feeling was the only thing that seemed to occupy his mind anymore. As soon as the euphoria was over, Austin immediately wanted more, and that was the state of mind he found himself in while sitting on that disgusting toilet. That's when Austin got an idea. If the curse was picking up steam and solidifying his blood at a more rapid pace, there surely had to be specks of it flowing throughout his entire body. That meant he could remove bits of the affliction from anywhere, and that's precisely what he aimed to do as he rolled up his right sleeve.

Austin ripped the freshly used blade over a patch of skin and let out a grunt of pain while blood poured from the wound. He impatiently waited for the hurt that rippled through his arm to disappear, and for it to be replaced with that magical feeling he so desperately craved. Suddenly, the sensation hit Austin out of nowhere and his whole body went limp as his senses were overwhelmed by pleasure. As he sat motionless on top of the public toilet, Austin had no idea what would kill him first, the curse or the blood loss, and he didn't care. He was absolutely fine with any kind of death, as long as he kept getting that otherworldly feeling of pleasure with each cut of his flesh.

Those of Eight

FLORENCE LET OUT A long sigh as she wiped the sweat from her brow. Even though dusk was fast approaching, the desert sun was still powerful enough to produce a tremendous amount of heat. She was thankful that she and her colleagues were in the shade, studying an interesting find towards the entrance of a cave, but they were not nearly far enough into the cavern to reap the full benefits. Florence pushed herself up off the large rock she had been sitting on and moved towards Professor Tillinghast. She made sure to avoid the large lamplight that was helping to illuminate the wall covered in cave writing that the professor was studying.

"Richard," she quietly said as she came up to her teacher. After a few moments of not receiving a reply, she reached out and gently touched his shoulder.

Tillinghast spun around in surprise, but upon seeing Florence's face he let out a light chuckle. "I'm sorry, my dear," he smiled. "You startled me."

"Professor," Florence cut straight to the point, "the others are starting to get a little restless. We've been in this cave all day." She leaned in close and whispered, "We're all wondering if you're close to wrapping this up."

"What?" Tillinghast sputtered as he took a step back. He pointed at the cave wall. "This is such an important discovery! It will take weeks to truly unravel the mystery of what these ancient words mean."

Florence slowly nodded. "That's nice and all... but I meant are you close to wrapping it up for the day?"

"Oh," Tillinghast blushed at the notion that he had completely misunderstood what Florence had meant. He quickly nodded. "I shouldn't be too much longer." Tillinghast pointed at Joey and Dione, who sat with their backs to the opposite wall of the cave, blank expressions on their faces. "I see that their energy has run out for the day," he said with a bit of amusement. He smiled at Florence. "Tell them we'll be out of here in less than an hour."

"Sounds good," Florence happily replied as she turned and walked back to her academic peers.

"So... how much longer?" Joey asked as Florence sat back down next to them.

"About an hour," she replied.

"An hour," Joey groaned. He dropped his head between his knees as he whined to himself.

"Hey, Professor!" Dione yelled out. "Can't you just put a pin in whatever you're looking at until tomorrow?"

Tillinghast kept his eyes focused on the inscribed writing as he replied, "Unfortunately not. I really must translate this last little bit of passage before we leave. It will make things a lot easier for us come tomorrow."

"What have you translated so far?" Florence asked as she squinted at the ancient writing.

"Not much I'm afraid," Tillinghast truthfully replied. "The writing is in a language I've never seen before, although... there are some distinct symbols that I can relate to other ancient languages." His inner archaeologist took over and he began explaining, "By taking each of the symbols on their own and finding the closest example from another language, I've been able to cobble together a few sentences; nothing too substantial though."

"Well, what do you have so far?" Dione inquired.

Tillinghast looked down at the small notepad in his hands as he recited, "For this land we have made home." He stood up as he looked for the next sentence he had fully translated. "Um… dark is the night… for hiding in the shadows… lives those of eight."

"Those of eight?" Florence repeated in a puzzled voice. "What the hell does that mean?"

Tillinghast shrugged his shoulders. "I have no idea." He turned back towards the wall covered in writing. "That's why I have to finish translating at least a few more words. Hopefully, there will be something that will give us a little more insight to what 'those of eight' means."

The sudden sound of skittering coming from off in the recesses of the cave drew everyone's attention towards the darkness. An eerie feeling muscled its way over the site as the last fading rays of the sun's light only worked to amplify the ominous sensation. The four sat there in silence as they each individually hoped it had been their imagination. Only a few seconds passed before another round of skittering sounded, this time growing slightly louder.

"What the hell was that?" Joey spat out in an uneven voice that broke the silence.

Tillinghast swallowed hard before replying, "It was probably just a bat." He gestured towards the mouth of the cave. "The sun is setting, so it's almost time for them to awaken."

Dione stumbled to his feet. "Well, I don't want to be around when that happens."

"Same," Joey nodded in agreement as he scrambled to snatch up his gear.

The four quickly started to collect their items, each eagerly not wanting to run into whatever was making the unsettling noises. Another round of skittering sounded, and now there was no mistaking that it had grown closer. Tillinghast froze with his hand halfway shoved into his pack. While the others moved about, he stared into the darkness of the cave that stretched out before him. The noise was drawing closer, and soon, whatever was in the darkness would be upon them.

"Professor!" Florence shouted.

"What?" Tillinghast muttered while he shook his head as if he was coming out of a daze.

"Stop staring into space and help pack up our tools," she frantically commanded.

"Of course," he mumbled. Tillinghast took in a deep breath. "I'm sorry for spacing out like that. It's just that... I believe the noises are drawing closer."

"All the more reason to get the hell out of here!" Dione shouted as he took the last of the tools near him and gently placed them into a carrying box.

Tillinghast turned and longingly examined the writing on the wall he was kneeling in front of. He felt something touch his shoulder and turned his gaze to see Florence giving him a gentle look. "It's just so incredible," Tillinghast slowly said in a solemn tone. "An ancient language from some long-lost civilization. A forgotten group of people, and a plethora of evidence pointing towards the notion that they occupied this cave for some time. It's the discovery of a lifetime... and we have to leave it behind."

"Just for now," Florence said as she held out a hand.

Tillinghast took it and rose to his feet. "I suppose you're right."

"We'll come back tomorrow," Florence said while turning towards the entrance, "I promise."

Joey grabbed his backpack and hustled for the mouth of the cave. He hollered over his shoulder, "Come on! Let's get out of here!"

He ran forward with Dione quickly in tow. Joey could begin to make out the night sky as he neared the exit. The small speckling of stars that were already present was a welcome sight. He picked up his speed a little as he neared the homestretch. Joey closed his eyes and outstretched his arms in anticipation of coming out of the cave. Yet, that didn't happen. Instead, he felt his body slam into something that stretched against the momentum he had been carrying with his run. Joey immediately opened his eyes to discover that the substance he had run into was a large mass of nearly invisible string. He desperately tried to pull back, but found that he couldn't break free from the substance.

"What's wrong?" Dione asked as he came to a stop just a few feet from Joey.

"There's some sort of string here!" Joey shouted. A wave of panic set in and he yelled, "I'm stuck! I can't get free from it."

Dione took a few tentative steps forward, which brought him close enough to just barely notice the strange material that had ensnared Joey. Curiosity got the better of Dione and he stepped up right next to his comrade, reaching his hand towards the mysterious substance.

"Don't touch it!" Joey yelled right as Dione's hand connected with a strand of the stuff.

"Oh crap!" Dione yelled as he tried to pull his finger away and found that he couldn't.

"What are you doing?" Florence growled as her and Tillinghast came up behind them. "Quit fooling around."

"Don't come any closer!" Joey frantically yelled. "There's something here! I don't know what it is, but it's sticky. I can't get out of it!"

Florence moved up next to Joey and examined the front part of his body to confirm that there was indeed something he was stuck against. She immediately realized that the substance wasn't string, but the only other possibility that came to her mind on what the mysterious material could be seemed impossible. The horrifying skittering was growing louder, drawing ever closer as the four sat mere inches from salvation. Florence studied the strands that Joey found himself stuck to. She followed each piece with her eyes and saw that they stretched out to both ends of the cave's exit. In fact, there was enough of the material that there was no way to get out without touching it in some way.

"Oh my god," Florence gasped while taking a small step back.

"What is it?" Tillinghast frantically inquired while he glanced over his shoulder towards the ever-closer skittering sound.

"I think it's..." Florence took in a deep breath before stammering, "I-I t-think it's a s-spider's web."

"That's impossible," Dione argued as he desperately tried to pull his hand free. "No spider could make something this big."

Suddenly, the skittering came to a stop, sounding as though it was less than a hundred feet from them. Florence and Tillinghast cautiously turned their gaze back toward the site. The lamplight was still turned on and illuminated the wall with the writings etched in it. A bit of movement just out of the corner of Florence's eye brought her attention to the top part of the wall. There were several tense moments where she waited, knowing something was just out of view. Then a human hand came into the light from the direction of the ceiling. It was quickly followed by another set of fingers and then the top of a person's head came into view.

"Who are you?" Florence called out.

In one fluid motion, the person scurried across the surface of the wall and into the light. Florence immediately noticed the four extra arms that were clearly covered in some type of strange hair. The person brought their head up to show eight pairs of eyes complete with a set of fangs that covered the area of the face where a mouth should have been. Florence and Tillinghast let out screams of horror as the abomination scurried further into view, revealing an elongated posterior that stretched out for several feet. The thing's legs were placed below the body, in a way that resembled the rear appendages of a spider.

"What the hell is happening?" Joey screamed in complete panic as he couldn't turn to see what was making its way towards them.

A dozen more sounds of skittering filled the cave and Florence noticed more movement coming from the illuminated wall. Several more horrific, human-spider hybrids emerged into view.

Tillinghast yelled out, "My god! That's what it meant." He was barely holding back tears as he screamed his realization. "'Those of eight'! It was talking about these things!" He turned to look at Florence, who immediately met his gaze. Tillinghast whispered in horror, "The people who created those etchings... this wasn't their home." He pointed at the monstrosities as they eagerly moved towards them. "It was theirs."

Mush Brain Fever

Marissa let out a gargled groan as she stared up at the ceiling of her bedroom. Her fever had somehow gotten worse from just a few hours ago, and it was so intense that she couldn't think straight. Every time she tried to say something, it would just come out as a stream of incomprehensible babble. Even if she could form a coherent sentence, no one would be able to hear it. Her husband, Jaxon, was still at work. So, she was left in the house by herself, only sharing the space with her cat, Whiskers.

The feline had tried to keep her company at first, snuggling up next to her, but then Marissa started to scream in agony. Of course, the cat did not enjoy all the intense noise and quickly scampered away. This left her alone in her bed with a raging fever that was quickly turning her brain into mush. To make matters worse, she was faced with a swirl of anger mixed with confusion, and she couldn't comprehend why she felt either. All she could do was groan from the horrible sensation that coursed through her body.

Hours of this endless cycle of pain and groaning continued, making the day drag to a near standstill. Her brow became soaked in sweat, which rolled off onto the sheets, making the bed damp and uncomfortable. Finally, there was a break in the madness when she felt a gurgling sensation building in her stomach. She flipped onto her left side and pointed her face towards the nearest wall. Marissa made the move just in time to projectile vomit a large stream onto the white wall. Mere moments after puking, a bit of comprehension came back to her. It wasn't much, but it was enough for her to stare at the bile that oozed down the wall and realize that something wasn't right. She had never spewed black vomit before, and yet, there it was dripping its way down the wall.

Marissa's puzzlement was quickly replaced by another surge in her temperature, seemingly setting her insides ablaze. She gasped in sudden agony and convulsed widely on top of her bed. Small bits of black vomit still clung to her lips, coming off on the sheets as she writhed in pain, but her attention was solely focused on the horrific fever that was ravaging her body and not the disgusting stains that were now sprinkled across her bed. As she seized about, Whiskers tentatively trotted into the room to give a small meow of concern. This was met with a loud grunt of agony from Marissa, who grabbed hold of a pillow and flung it across the room.

As Whiskers ran back out of the room in a panic, she desperately tried to understand what was happening, but her brain had once again returned to a nonfunctioning state. She continued to widely fling her arms about, not realizing it when she punched a hole clean through the sheetrock of the wall her bedrest lay against. Marissa felt a terrible fear grip her stomach as she flung herself about. She had not felt pain anywhere near this level before in her life. Her mind was completely convinced that there was a good chance she would die from whatever the horrible illness was.

Eventually, her temperature died down and the pain gradually subsided. Merely being in a position where she wasn't in constant agony brought her into a state of euphoria. She felt so light, it was as though she was lying on nothing but air. Marissa was able to fall in and out of sleep over the next hour or so. Her eyes periodically snapped open to stare around for a few moments before immediately closing. On several occasions, she awoke to find a bird's eye view of her bed without her body in it. She dismissed those moments as nothing more than a strange bit of lucid dreaming before hurdling back into unconsciousness.

When she eventually came out of her nap, the effects of the fever seemed to be all but gone. In place of agony, Marissa was left with a hunger that caused her stomach to roar, as well as being hit by a lethargic feeling that made each bit of movement seem like it took all her strength to perform it. As she made her way to the kitchen in search of something to eat, she realized that her mind was finally thinking clearly. With a fully functioning brain, she began the long process of piecing the previous night's events together.

She distinctly remembered heading out to a nearby club with a few of her friends from her office. They were celebrating someone getting a large promotion, though Marissa couldn't remember who all was in the group, or even whose promotion it was for that matter. Little bits and pieces started to come back to her, but it was a jumbled mess. She heard small bits of a bumping bassline inside her head, then recalled flashing lights as she moved about the crowded club. Suddenly, she remembered the searing pain in her neck, instinctively placing her hand over the area that had hurt the night before.

Marissa ran her fingers along her smooth skin until coming to a stop on two small indents in her neck. She immediately made a detour to the bathroom to examine the problem area in the mirror. Marissa cranked her head off to the right, which barely allowed her to make out the anomalies on her neck. The more she studied the area, the more she began to realize that she was looking at two bite marks. But that didn't make any sense to her as she hadn't been around any animals who would have caused something like what she saw in the mirror.

She decided to just ignore the marks for the moment and focused on finding something to eat. Marissa made her way to the kitchen in a very gradual manner, taking note that she was losing a great deal of energy with each step. By the time she had reached the door to her fridge, she felt like she was going to collapse. She threw open the door and peered across the refrigerated items for something appealing. Yet, as her eyes scanned everything, she felt a sick sensation in the pit of her stomach. Food she would normally love to enjoy in a guilt-free manner did not seem appealing at all to her at that moment. She frantically dug around inside the fridge, but still found herself coming up short at finding anything appetizing.

Marissa also noticed that even the smell of the food was unpleasant and she took a few steps back from the fridge. Then, a random odor floating through the air caught her attention. She had never smelt anything like it, but she found it incredibly pleasing. Like an animal, she sniffed the air around her trying to locate the source of the aroma, moving her head about in each direction. Eventually, she finally realized where the scent was coming from as she stared down at Whiskers. *Eat him,* her mind suddenly whispered to her. She felt a stab of guilt form in her gut for even thinking of the unspeakable action that had flashed through her brain, and yet, there was still something there, drawing her towards her cat.

An urge bubbled up inside of Marissa, and she found it difficult to fight back. Her mouth watered as she stepped towards the feline. Whiskers didn't make a mad dash or even try to move as she bent down and picked him up. The cat was completely calm as she held him in her arms, slowly stroking his head. She could feel her cat's steady heart rate, the rhythmic beating called out to her. Whiskers didn't even know that something was wrong until the first bite, but by then, it was too late for an escape.

In drawing that first bit of blood, Marissa turned into a savage beast. She lost control for several minutes, entering a period of blackout. When her brain kicked back on, she immediately let out a gasp of horror as a puddle of crimson covered the floor directly in front of her with Whiskers placed squarely in the middle of it. The horrible truth of what she had done hit her square in the gut and she fell on her knees. How could she have done something like that? It was truly unforgivable. Yet, at least physically, she didn't feel bad at all. In fact, Marissa sensed a new surge of energy coursing through her. She felt incredible, like she could take on a hundred men. This glorious sensation was short-lived as the sound of the front door opening caused her heart to fall into her stomach.

"I'm home, babe!" Jaxon shouted as he took off his shoes in the entryway.

She panicked as she rightly assumed that Jaxon would not be all too happy to find that she had ripped apart their cat. She racked her brain on what to do, but couldn't come up with any definitive plan, so Marissa simply managed to stumble to her feet as Jaxon entered the kitchen. There was a look of shock that crossed her husband's face as he scanned the carnage laid out before him. She didn't know what to say, so the two stood there in complete silence.

"W-what the h-hell?" Jaxon finally stuttered in terror. "What happened here?"

"I can explain," Marissa frantically blurted out as she took a step forward. She felt hurt as she witnessed the sight of her husband backtracking into the living room, but upon noticing that blood covered her hands, she didn't blame him.

She wanted to give Jaxon some explanation of what happened, some fantastic answer that would make everything okay, but she knew she couldn't. Marissa had done something terrible, simply because she had given into an animalistic urge that certainly wasn't worth it. She understood that in hindsight. Yet, even though she was racked with guilt as her husband stared at her in horror, she couldn't help but notice an incredible scent permeating the air. Marissa gave a few quick sniffs to pinpoint the smell, which she quickly found to be coming from Jaxon. She gasped in shock as she realized what her body was trying to goad her into doing. Marissa felt terrible about even thinking of such a thing... but then her mouth started to water.

That Which Belongs to the Sea

"You don't have to do this!" Josiah shouted as he struggled against his bonds.

"Of course I don't!" Philbrook yelled over the crashing waves, "But I want to, so I will!"

Josiah looked to Mac, who shared his feeling of despair. The two men were hopelessly tied up in the small, wooden rowboat. Neither one was able to loosen the ropes that bound their hands and feet. The turbulent ocean waves slammed against the small boat, and Josiah found himself holding his breath with each strike. All it would take was a powerful wave to capsize the boat and send them to the depths below.

Philbrook laughed from the deck of the Monstrum with several of his crew. Schneider, his first mate, stood off to the side keeping watch over the rocky waters for any sign of creatures. The wind constantly swept over the two boats with unrelenting intensity. Josiah heard thunder crack overhead and said a silent prayer for the storm to be over quickly. He also prayed that the rope connecting his little rowboat to the Monstrum would hold.

Josiah took a deep breath before giving another go at stopping Philbrook from actually going through with his insane plan. "You don't have to do this!" he shouted. "I promise we won't tell anyone about this!"

"Of course you won't," Philbrook laughed. "You'll be dead."

"We don't have to be," Josiah yelled. "There's still time to pull us back in."

"No!" Philbrook angrily screamed and shook his head. "You think this is the first time we've done this?" The captain let his crew laugh before shouting, "We've done this dozens of times! The location isn't the same, but our methods are!"

"You son of a bitch!" Josiah screamed. "How many people have you killed!"

"Dozens," Philbrook smirked, "but it has made us all quite a bit of money." He tapped his prosthetic left hand against the railing of the ship. "That's how I could afford this ship, as well as my arm. All we have to do is lure some fresh-faced kid looking for adventure out on the seas with us, slather an old rowboat in fish blood, tie them up, and then push them out onto the waters."

"So you do this just to catch some sharks?" Josiah shouted in horror.

"Not sharks, my boy." Philbrook shook his head, "What lives in this part of the sea is far more magnificent and terrifying than any shark."

Schneider chimed in, "The things we've caught are scarier than your worst nightmares. We've seen things out here that you couldn't even dream of!"

"You're disgusting!" Josiah screamed. "Every last one of you deserves to die!"

"Well, in that case, you'll have to include your friend with you," Philbrook chuckled.

Josiah slowly turned his head toward Mac. He looked him in the eyes as he asked, "Did you know they were doing this?"

Mac hung his head. "I did."

Josiah kicked Mac with his tied feet. "You're no better than them!"

"You're probably right," Mac shouted over the waves, "but I'm the only one who realized that it needed to stop."

"How long?" Josiah asked. When Mac didn't answer he shouted, "How long did it take you? How many people did you help this disgusting man kill?"

"Seven," Mac shamefully responded.

"You killed seven men!" Josiah screamed in rage.

"Oh, we've sacrificed a lot more than that," Philbrook shouted. He pointed at Mac, "He only knows about the seven, but there have been more."

"All of this, just to make a few bucks?" Josiah shouted.

"It ain't just a few bucks, boy," Philbrook yelled. "A twenty-foot creature that has never been seen before fetches a high price on the black market." He cackled, "There's no reason why these abominations should get to swim around without anyone making a profit off of them."

"What about what you said to me?" Josiah shouted, "'Don't desecrate or hoard that which belongs to the sea'!"

"Damn the sea!" Philbrook shouted in anger. He slammed his prosthetic hand against the railing as he yelled, "The sea takes what it wants from us without asking. So why shouldn't we from it?" He continued his rant, "The sea desecrated me when it took my hand! It took my brother without a second thought. These waters have ripped too much from me and my crew! So why shouldn't we take from it?"

"Because nature has a way of punishing those who take more than they should!" Josiah shouted in response.

"Grab me my harpoon gun!" Philbrook screamed. "I'll kill this cocky son of a bitch myself!"

"I saw something peeking out of the waves, Captain!" Schneider shouted.

Philbrook waited for one of his crew members to bring him the harpoon gun and then moved over to Schneider. He peered out at the waves in search of his next catch. After a few moments of nothing, he yelled, "Damn it, Schneider! There's nothing there."

Something suddenly slammed against the bottom right side of the boat. The Monstrum leaned to the side for a moment before balancing out. Philbrook felt a rush go through him as a confident smile spread across his face. He made his way over to the left side of the boat anticipating that the creature would show up there. The captain patiently waited alongside two of his crew for the thing to show itself. From where they were on the deck, no one could see the dozens of tentacles slowly creeping up the sides of the ship.

Josiah spotted the appendages of the beast and immediately knew that the creature was well over twenty feet in length. He feared the thing would drag the Monstrum down below the surface, which would take him and Mac with it. He turned to see the terror-filled eyes of Mac as he also looked on. That's when he realized that now would be the best chance they had to escape.

"Mac!" he shouted over the storm. "This is our chance!"

"There's no way," Mac responded in despair. "That thing is going to rip us apart!"

"No, it won't," Josiah insisted. "We're too small for it. That's why it's focused on the Monstrum. This gives us a chance to get out of here while everyone else is distracted."

"Alright," Mac nodded. "It's worth a shot, I suppose."

"Move so we're back to back," Josiah ordered. He waited until he felt his fellow hostage pressing up against his back before saying, "Now try to untie my hands."

While the two men desperately tried to break free in the rowboat, the crew of the Monstrum still waited for the sea creature to reveal itself to them. Philbrook held his harpoon gun at the ready as he gestured for the closest crewmember to peek over the railing. The man silently nodded and inched forward. Before the crewmember had made it that far, a giant tentacle flew up over the side of the ship. It moved forward with tremendous speed and the top of it slammed the crewmember to the ground.

"Help!" the man screamed in terror.

The tentacle ripped itself back from the crewmember, taking a large chunk of his flesh with him. The man grabbed the circle-shaped divot in his chest and screamed in agony as he flailed on the deck. Philbrook looked to see the tentacle hovering close to the man. It was then that he noticed a circular mouth on the front of the appendage. After a few more seconds of starring, he was able to see the hundreds of sharp teeth that lined the orifice.

Before anyone moved, the tentacle shot back down and latched itself onto the wounded crewmember's abdomen. The sickening sound of ripping flesh occurred as the tentacle pulled itself back. The crewmember gasped in pain as blood spurted from the open wound. The man reached out a hand towards Philbrook for help, but he just stood there in shock. The tentacle wrapped itself around the unfortunate soul's left leg and started to drag him across the deck. With a quick scream, the man was pulled over the edge and into the sea.

An instant later there were almost a dozen tentacles that shot up the sides of the boat. One of the crewmembers tried to swing a machete at an appendage but missed. He was rapidly descended upon by several tentacles that ripped off large chunks of his body. Philbrook backed away in horror as the man fell to his knees. The doomed individual desperately pressed his hands against two of the newly torn holes in him. Philbrook saw the pleading look on the crewmember's face as a tentacle slowly wrapped itself around him. There was nothing that could be done as the man was pulled through the air and out of sight.

Mac finally was able to untie the ropes around Josiah's hands. With his hands free, Josiah frantically undid the knots around his feet. He spun around and began to work on the bindings for his accomplice's hands. The sound of screams brought his attention back toward the boat where he saw one of the crew being ripped apart by the mouths of the tentacles. He shuddered in horror as he kept working on the ropes. Finally, he managed to get the knots loose and pulled the ropes free of Mac's hands.

"Undo your feet!" he shouted.

Josiah turned towards the Monstrum and the rope that was keeping them attached to it. He frantically tugged at the knot with all his might as the waves slammed into the side of the small boat. With a final tug, he pulled the knot free and realized there was a metal chain attached to it. He followed the chain with his eyes and found that it was welded to the side of the boat.

"We're still attached!" Josiah yelled.

Mac turned to see what he meant and noticed the chain. "Oh no, I forgot about that!"

"What do we do?"

"We can't do anything," Mac replied. "There's nothing in here that can cut through metal. Our only hope is that, that thing won't sink the Monstrum."

Josiah looked up to the deck of the ship and noticed that only Philbrook and Schneider were left. One of the tentacles flew towards the captain, but he managed to shoot off his harpoon in time. The weapon stabbed directly through the appendage, and it fell back against the railing of the ship. The tentacle sat on the railing for a moment before falling over the side of the vessel. On the way down, the appendage slammed into the metal chain and broke one of the links off. The force of the enormous limb slamming against the chain sent the rowboat forward in the water a few feet, almost knocking Josiah over the side.

Mac caught and pulled him towards the center of the rowboat before he could fall into the water. Josiah gave him a nod as he looked back up towards the deck of the Monstrum. He witnessed two tentacles wrapping themselves around Schneider as he screamed out for help. The dual appendages started to move apart in opposite directions, slowly stretching Schneider out as they went. There was a brief moment where the first mate just hung there in between the tentacles, before he was forcefully ripped in half.

Josiah turned his focus towards the impending end of the captain as several tentacles started to move towards him. Philbrook aimed and shot another harpoon that managed to pin one of the tentacles to the deck. The other appendages quickly shot forward and enveloped the captain. Josiah couldn't see what was happening, but he could hear the screams of agony. After a few seconds, the limbs dispersed, and there was nothing but a blood stain left where Philbrook had been standing.

"Jesus Christ!" Mac muttered. "It ripped him to pieces."

"He got what he deserved," Josiah said as he turned towards Mac. "They all got what they deserved."

A sound of crunching metal brought Josiah's attention back towards the Monstrum. The tentacles were all slamming down across the ship, breaking the vessel into dozens of pieces. He watched as the ship was rapidly broken up and quickly disappeared beneath the waves.

Josiah shouted, "Thank god we're not attached to it anymore." A feeling of relief filled him as he noticed they were drifting away from the wreckage. He turned back to Mac. "Now all we have to worry about is waiting out the storm."

"And sharks," Mac shouted.

"What?"

"There are sharks in these waters. We have to keep a lookout and hope we don't attract any of them."

Josiah remembered that Philbrook had said he soaked the sides of the rowboat with fish blood. He slowly sat down as the feeling of relief quickly evaporated. Finally, he realized how hopeless their situation was as the waves slammed against the side of the boat. Thunder continued to sound overhead as the two silently sat there in despair.

Inside the Film

THE SUDDEN LIGHTS BLINDED Deshaun, causing him to grunt in pain as he closed his eyes. Though he couldn't see anything, he knew exactly what was happening. He waited as his eyes slowly adjusted while the two people behind him had already begun talking to each other. Once he was able to open his eyes without any sense of pain, he separated himself from the other two. He walked to the front of the room, making his way to the giant piece of see-through glass that blocked his escape.

Deshaun peered through the glass, out into the landscape of a normal, middle-class living room. He spotted a brown coffee table with kids' toys sprinkled around it, as well as a black recliner tucked in the corner off to his left side. Yet, more important than those things, he noticed the bald man with a beer gut sitting by himself on the couch. He could easily see the glare the man was shooting his way, letting him know he had to say something fast.

"Wait!" Deshaun screamed. "Don't turn off the TV! I'm trapped in here!"

The man's expression changed to one of confusion, but Deshaun could tell he had piqued the stranger's interest because the man had sat up a little.

"I know it sounds crazy," Deshaun continued while lowering his volume, "but I've been stuck in this movie for weeks."

"Huh," the man chuckled, "this one must have built in some of those new, interactive features."

"It's not a feature!" Deshaun yelled. He saw the man start to lean back to his original position on the couch, which was a strong signal that he was losing him. "What's your name?" he asked.

The man stared for a second before letting out a sigh and lifting the remote to change the channel.

Deshaun frantically yelled, "You! The bald guy on the white couch, what's your name?"

The stranger blinked in surprise before looking down at his furniture to double-check that the piece of furniture he was sitting on was indeed white. After stroking his chin for a moment, the man lightly shrugged before responding, "Michael."

"Okay, Michael," Deshaun took in a deep breath. "This is going to be a lot to unpack, but you have to believe me. I've been stuck inside this movie for weeks now. You see… I accidentally pissed off a sorcerer. I sold him some bad investments, and to get back at me he conjured up this spell that keeps me trapped in this garbage flick from the fifties."

"This is getting a little too weird," Michael grumbled.

"Look man, you gotta believe me!" Deshaun pleaded, "I need you! I can't get out of here without your help. I have to get someone willing to release me from this nightmare!"

Michael sat on the couch in silence for a moment before shaking his head. "Nah," he said while lifting the remote, "I'm not feeling it."

"No!" Deshaun screamed while banging his hands against the glass.

Suddenly, everything went dark as the large piece of glass disap-peared. Deshaun stood there in com-plete stillness for several moments before falling to his knees. He burst into tears as the characters from the film silently watched.

"Why, why, why!" Deshaun blubbered. "Why'd it have to be this movie? I hate this movie!"

Everybody Loves Ice Cream

Tommy loved ice cream. Then again, what ten-year-old child didn't? The thought of the frozen treat swirled through his mind on that hot, summer day, as the July sun was especially brutal with the penetrating rays bombarding Tommy. Sweat poured down his cheeks, falling off in dozens of tiny, salt-filled droplets. He walked down the empty sidewalk in his quiet, suburban neighborhood. There was little commotion to be had, as it was well into the workday. Every adult in the area had driven off to their nine-to-five, leaving the neighborhood children to their own devices.

Though, on this particular week, Tommy was in a more isolated situation than normal. The environment in which he found himself arose from almost all of the local parents growing fearful of the idea of what their children would do if allowed to roam the streets wild and free. This created a large surge of adolescents shipped off to the nearest summer camp for a two-week period. There was but one exception to this way of thinking: Tommy's parents. They knew that he was not a troublemaker, much less a child who would wander far from the house. The cost of giving him a few bucks a day for two weeks was far less than the cost of sending him to any local summer camp.

In pure desperation, Tommy had been walking around since early in the morning in the hopes that he would happen upon some other unfortunate child such as himself. Though, as the minutes ticked by, his hopes were declining at an exponential rate. Not to mention the growing heat of the sun was really beginning to get to him. His feet left the sidewalk, crossing through the grass to the left side of him. He jumped off the few inches of raised ground onto the actual pavement of the road, took in a deep breath, and allowed himself to fall backward, landing with a plop in the grass of some random person's yard.

Tommy needed a moment to sit to counteract the scorching heat. The idea of ice cream became more enticing to him with each passing second. *I would do anything for some ice cream*, he thought to himself. At this point, he would have taken any flavor that was thrown at him: vanilla, chocolate, strawberry. Hell, he probably would have even given sherbet a genuine try. Despite the desperation he felt, Tommy knew he would be perfectly fine if he could just get back home, where there was a large pint of rocky road with his name on it.

Unfortunately, in his aimless wandering, he had landed himself a good fifteen-minute walk from his house. Since there was no other alternative, it seemed as though he would be making a long, overheated walk back home. Slowly, Tommy lifted his back off the grass and let out a heavy sigh. As he rose to his feet, he let out an audible groan. He stretched his arms into the air, feeling his muscles grow taut in the upper part of his body.

"I guess I better start walking," he muttered to himself out loud.

His feet begin to move him in the direction of his house, with each foot almost dragging upon the ground. It had not been but a few seconds when a distant noise slipped into his ears. Tommy scanned in every direction trying to find the source of the growing sound. Even if it was a faint noise through the humid air, he could recognize that iconic melody anywhere. It was an ice cream van!

Straining his ears to hear, Tommy was able to determine that the music was coming from somewhere in front of him. He jogged forward, not wishing to spend another minute without ice-cold relief in his hands. Newly invigorated by the prospect of an approaching treat, Tommy progressed forward with a rapidly increasing pace, the music growing louder as he did so. *That's weird,* he thought to himself, *the music doesn't sound right.* He knew his hearing was probably a bit off due to his jogging, but the music seemed different from what he was normally accustomed to.

Tommy stopped for a moment, wanting to listen more intently, as well as take a quick rest. Even though he had stopped jogging, the music continued to grow louder, as though the vehicle was headed straight for him. He took a moment to glance around him at the stillness that filled the area before a question popped into his head. *What is an ice cream truck doing here?* It was a fair question to ponder considering there were no children in the neighborhood at the moment, as had been the case for the past several days as well. Surely any ice cream man would have entered the neighborhood earlier in the week and found that out.

Just as those ideas began to occupy Tommy's mind, something crept into view at the corner of his peripheral vision from far off down the street. A large, dark vehicle slowly drove over the asphalt in his direction. The vehicle's slow pace made him tense up, setting an uneasy feeling loose inside of him. He stared at the strange vehicle, trying to ascertain what it was. It wasn't until the vehicle was a few hundred feet from him that he realized it was indeed an ice cream van. At least... he was fairly sure it was. Tommy had never seen an ice cream van that wasn't white, yet the one coming towards him looked like it had been painted black.

Eventually, the van moved close enough to Tommy for it to be made abundantly clear that something was wrong with the music. The song played at the normal speed that he was used to, but all the notes were far lower than usual, giving the tune an unsettling tone. After another minute or so of petering along, the van finally pulled up directly in front of him. This also seemed weird to him, as he was on one of the main streets of the neighborhood. He had never seen an ice cream van stop on a main street before. Normally, the ice cream man would pull onto a side street, so children wouldn't be in danger of traffic.

Tommy stood there, looking over the unconventional vehicle before him. With it directly in front of him, he was able to confirm that the van had been sloppily painted black, as bits of white were visible through the uneven coats that had been slapped on the sides of the vehicle. The paint was also chipping in various areas across the surface of the van. He eventually brought his attention upward to find a large, fake ice cream cone sitting on the roof. It was extremely worn, with several large chunks missing from it, exposing the weird materials that had been used to craft the large ornament. But the part he found most unsettling was the opening where the driver would appear. It was pitch black, with him not being able to make out a single detail of the interior of the vehicle.

Tommy took a timid step towards the vehicle, all the while psyching himself up to speak. "Hello?" he called into the van. "Is anyone in there?"

The van engine immediately cut off, causing the music to abruptly stop. This startled Tommy, causing him to jump back a bit. Silence quickly filled the air, adding another layer to the uneasiness that he was already feeling. Several moments went by, and yet, there was no noise coming from the van. No sound of movement, or even a hint that someone was in the vehicle. Tommy was just about to turn away when something began to come forward out of the darkness of the van. A gargantuan hand slowly crossed the threshold of the opening into the light of the small counter. The enormous appendage was certainly larger than Tommy's head, and it easily made his dad's hands look like those of a small child in comparison.

The fingers of the hand stretched out, tapping themselves repeatedly against the counter. Tommy could have sworn that each finger was at least eight inches long, with the palm being in proportion to them. Tommy just stood gawking at the massive hand before him. He was so transfixed by it that he didn't even notice the index finger tapping in an impatient manner. The hand finally lifted off the counter, forming into a fist before slamming itself back down onto the solid material. The loud noise was enough to break Tommy from the daze he had been in, and in response, the hand relaxed, letting its palm lay flat on the counter with the fingers stretched out again.

At this point, Tommy just wanted to get the first thing he could find on a menu and get away from the van as quickly as possible. He frantically scanned the van again, desperately looking for any sort of signage. To his dismay, there wasn't a single bit of art or writing to be found on the surface of the vehicle. Tommy stuck his hand in his pocket, fumbling around to pull out whatever bit of money was clumped together in there. He yanked out a random amount, taking a glance at it to find it was only three dollars and some change.

"I hope this is enough," he muttered under his breath. The worrying thought of not having enough to actually buy anything only added even more anxiety to Tommy's troubled mind. He gently sat the money down on the counter in front of the gigantic hand. "One vanilla cone," he said, with a noticeable trembling in his voice.

Without a single word, the hand moved over the money, slowly lowering itself onto the worn currency before dragging it backward, disappearing with it into the darkness. Tommy stood there, with only the sound of a light breeze blowing by him. After several minutes, the hand reappeared, clutching a cone that looked miniscule in its grasp. He stepped forward, tentatively reaching out to grab the treat. As he took hold of the cone, he realized the treat was actually much larger than he had initially thought, with it even taking him two hands to hold the ice cream properly.

Even with the treat in hand, he still felt uneasy about the enormous hand and the worn-down van, so he turned away as quickly as possible. He walked at a normal pace for a few steps before breaking into a fast walk to hustle away from the van. As he moved, he heard the engine sputter and turn on behind him. He would breathe a sigh of relief once the van was far away from him. While he anxiously waited for the van to drive, Tommy took a small lick of the ice cream to calm his nerves, to which he immediately spat out in disgust. The treat was the blandest thing that he had ever tasted, with its flavor being akin to licking a piece of paper.

The horrible taste had distracted Tommy long enough to keep him from a more important matter. Bringing his mind back to the world around him, he noticed something was wrong. A sense of overwhelming dread washed over him and was quickly accompanied by a chill creeping up his spine. That horrible feeling was caused by the realization that the noise of the van's engine hadn't moved farther away from him, even though he had been continuously walking away from it. Slowly, trying his best not to turn his head, he looked out of the corner of his right eye. The sight of the van directly behind him sent a tidal wave of panic throughout his body.

To add even more unease to the situation, the van was driving in reverse in order to slowly creep along behind him. Tommy turned his attention back to the area in front of him and frantically scanned it for any way to escape. He noticed that a side road was coming up on his left. *He won't follow me onto the side road,* he thought to reassure himself. Coming up on the turn, he meticulously stepped with a slow and precise pace, so as to not let his movements give away the overwhelming panic that coursed through his body.

As Tommy made his way past the driveway of the first house on the side street, he heard the van come to a stop on the main street, giving him the impression he had made the driver lose their nerves. He let out a small sigh of relief while he continued to walk at the precise and deliberate pace, he had been moving at to be on the safe side. Suddenly, the noise of tires moving across asphalt sounded as the van slowly crept onto the side street with him. To make the situation even more unnerving, when Tommy glanced over his shoulder to see where the vehicle was, he saw that the van was still moving in reverse.

Suddenly, the vehicle sped up for a second, before immediately slowing down once it had pulled up directly beside him. Tommy came to an abrupt stop, out of fear more than anything, to which the van responded in kind by slamming on its brakes. This brought a silence to the side road as he and the van silently stood there, mere feet from each other. Tommy desperately wished for the whole situation to be over. He wanted more than anything for the van to just disappear into thin air, but he knew that wasn't going to happen. So, Tommy swallowed hard to help relieve some of the irritation in his dry throat as he prepared to try to talk with the driver of the ice cream van.

"C-c-c-an I help you?" Tommy barely managed to stutter out.

In response to his question, the hand emerged from the opening in the vehicle, shaking an index finger menacingly at him. The gesture froze him in place, afraid of what would come next. Was this random creep going to yell at him? The answer was no. That was far from what was to come next. As if to officially break the silence, a low noise began to sound from inside the van, which Tommy quickly identified as a strange moan. Gradually, the noise began to grow louder in volume, slowly morphing into a shriek. It was a sound that was reminiscent of someone trying to suck in a large breath of air while forcing a yell out at the same time.

The shriek continued to grow in volume, reaching deafening levels as it grew less human-sounding by the second. Tommy threw his ice cream onto the ground and covered his ears in a futile attempt to shield them from the horrible sound. Despite his efforts, the inhuman shrieks still broke through the makeshift barrier, bringing pain to his ear drums. In the middle of the horrific sounds, the enormous hand slammed itself down upon the counter, spreading its fingers out. He watched as it began to seize, jerking about with random spasms, flopping about like a live fish dropped onto the deck of a sailing ship. The shriek continued to rise, causing utter agony to his ears.

He closed his eyes, trying to find some way to stop the attack on his ears. After several moments with them shut, he forced his eyes open to the sight of the enormous hand, which seemed to have changed in appearance. It was fairly hard to tell for sure with it flopping about, but the appendage seemed to have lost its color. The skin was turning from a normal fleshy tone to a gray, dull one. Suddenly, one of the fingers shot out of the hand, stretching itself several feet out from the rest of the hand. Just as Tommy had fully absorbed the image of a finger stretched far beyond its means, another of the hand's digits followed suit. Soon, all five of the fingers were stretched out, hanging limply like rubber hosing over the opening of the van.

He noticed that each finger now lacked any knuckles, and the distinguishing features of the stretched appendages had diminished. The surface of them was now unsettlingly smooth, making the fingers appear far more inhuman. Each finger was now at least four feet in length, with them continuing to elongate in size. Tommy shifted his gaze towards the center of the hand to discover that it had significantly shrunk in size. He watched as the mass of the hand continued to shrink, seemingly passing itself along to the ever-growing fingers.

As if finally reaching the desired length, the appendages began to grow in width, with each one growing out by three or four inches. The center of the hand was all but gone at that point, as the fingers continued to widen, making it nearly impossible for him to determine the true size of the appendages. To Tommy, they had completely stopped looking like fingers and now were more reminiscent of tentacles. While all this was happening, the shrieking still persisted, wailing away at Tommy's eardrums. The newly forming tentacles suddenly began to move, each with erratic patterns that made it seem like they were all moving autonomously from one another.

Then, the final piece of the nightmare started to take shape as an object began to grow from the tips of each of the tentacles. Through the pain, Tommy forced himself to take a closer look to see what was pushing forth from the ends of the tentacles. The new attributes looked like some type of razor-sharp claw, with each one almost three inches long and still growing. It didn't take long for him to notice that these seemed much sharper than ordinary claws. The claws' sharpness made them resemble knives in some ways. Knives that could easily tear through someone's flesh.

Suddenly, the horrible noise ceased while the now fully formed tentacles still whipped about, showing off the nearly foot-long daggers at the end of them. Tommy uncovered his ears, not even realizing until he did so that he had been breathing heavily. With the utmost care possible, he took a small step backward. His foot came down upon a small twig with a slight crunch emitting from it. One of the tentacles immediately shot through the air, stabbing the ground mere inches from his foot. Tommy felt his fight or flight instinct take over as he bolted away, sprinting as fast as his legs could carry him.

The loud noise began to scream from the van, as it spun around and started driving forward. Tommy's feet pounded down the sidewalk as his muscles strained to move him as fast as possible. He needed somewhere to go, otherwise he would be crushed under the vehicle that was speeding after him. His eyes franticly darted around, searching for something to get him out of the dire situation. That's when he spied a large, wooden fence just a few hundred feet from where he was. He immediately headed towards it, moving even faster than before.

The van continued its pursuit of him, gaining significant ground with each passing second. Tommy could feel the tentacles getting closer, moving in range to strike him. He looked over his shoulder to discover that the van was only a dozen or so feet behind him, while the house with the fence was but a few strides away. He bounded the last few steps, then leapt forward with all his might. Tommy flung himself far enough that his hands were able to grab hold of the top of the fence.

The van screeched to a sudden stop, with its opening only a few feet from him and the fence he clung to. One of the tentacles reared back ready to strike. Tommy flexed his arm muscles, pulling his body up. Driven by pure adrenaline, he heaved himself up, balancing on top of the fence with his stomach pushing into the wood. The tentacle sliced forward, hitting the part of the fence where he had just been. It smashed a sizable hole straight through the fence, sending wood fragments into the air. Tommy rolled over the top of the fence, falling into the guarded yard. He managed to bring his feet down just in time so they hit the ground first, while the force of the fall caused his body to follow immediately after.

Tommy's body violently rolled several feet into the yard before coming to a stop. He lay there in a daze for a moment, just staring up at the sky as he tried to recover some of his strength. His lungs felt like they were on fire, making it a lot harder for him to take in the oxygen he so desperately needed. Tommy felt like he wouldn't be able to breathe properly for the next hour, but that quickly changed once he heard the sounds of the van's engine stop. He sat up and intently listened for any movement coming from the other side of the fence.

Several moments of silence passed before he heard the door to the van squeak open. He could hear the creaking as something stepped out of the van and scrapped across the asphalt as it moved towards the fence. Tommy took a deep breath and held it, not wanting the creature to hear him. He heard a deep growl emanating from a few feet in front of him as all five of the tentacles slithered over the fence, stopping halfway down it. It felt as though they were all looking at Tommy, sizing up how best to rip him apart. Another growl came from over the fence, this one angrier than the one before. Slowly but surely, each tentacle withdrew back over the fence and out of view.

Tommy slowly let his held breath out when he heard the van engine turn over. He listened as the vehicle pulled away, moving further from the house. He sat there for several more minutes, still trying to pull himself together. Eventually, Tommy picked himself up, brushing the grass off his legs. He had to figure out where he was. Tommy made his way over to the fence and lifted himself up so he could peak over the top. He scanned the area for any familiar landmarks, eventually spying a bend in the street he had walked on many times before. He was maybe ten minutes from his home.

With as much caution as possible, Tommy meticulously pulled himself back over the fence. He had to use all the strength in his arms to lower himself slowly to the ground, so as to make as little sound as possible. No matter what, he had to make sure he wasn't found by the thing in the ice cream van. He would have to move quietly and care-fully, which would take much more time. Tommy started moving slowly through yards, letting the soft grass muffle his steps. By employing a slight crouch as he moved, Tommy was able to make himself much smaller than normal, which also helped to quiet his movements.

The process was extremely slow and painful. Every minute sound made Tommy freeze in absolute fear. The slight blow of the wind tied knots into his stomach with the horrible thought that the creature from the ice cream van could be right behind him. Cold sweat poured down his forehead while he took each terror-filled step. Finally, Tommy reached the house right before the left onto his street. He pressed himself against the wooden fence nearest to him, making sure to obscure anyone's view of him, while at the same time it also prevented him from scoping out his street.

Tommy took his time to cover the small distance to the end of the fence, hesitating with each tiny step. Once he had reached the final bit of wooden planks, he took a deep breath before spinning around the corner. To Tommy's relief, the street was empty, giving him a clean shot to his house. He took off at full speed, running for his front door. Tommy bounded down his street moving at a dead sprint. His house was the second one on the right, just a few hundred feet in front of him. As he quickly approached his place, Tommy heard a noise that sent chills running up his spine: the sound of an engine turning over.

He frantically scanned the street to see the ice cream truck pulling out of the driveway of one of the end houses. His adrenaline immediately kicked in, giving him an extra boost. The van moved forward, picking up speed as well. Tommy reached his lawn and darted across it, quickly bounding up his front steps. He reached out his left hand and wrapped his fingers around the doorknob.

Just as he was about to pull open the door, he felt something around his waist. He slowly peered down to see a tentacle wrapped around him. Tommy desperately tried to grab the doorknob with his other hand just as the tentacle pulled back. The force from the pull ripped him back, taking the doorknob with him.

"No, no, no!" Tommy screamed as he was pulled across the lawn and into the side opening of the van.

The vehicle slightly shook from left to right, filled with Tommy's screams. Then, the screaming came to an abrupt stop as the shaking of the vehicle came to a halt. There was silence in the neighborhood, except for the light wisps of the gentle breeze blowing through. Several more moments of silence passed before the engine of the van started up. The vehicle moved forward, turning off the road and making its way elsewhere.

***

Taylor felt a drop of sweat drip onto her cheek as she took in several deep breaths.

"It's so hot out here," she said to herself.

Her ears perked up at the faint sound of a familiar melody filled the air, which immediately picked up her spirits. She could really use some ice cream. *That's weird,* she thought to herself, *why does the music sound... lower than it normally is?*

Brewed with Extra Blood

Daniel sharply turned the wheel of his car when he realized he was about to pass the entrance to his neighborhood. He let out a sigh of relief and muttered to himself, "I drank a little too much tonight."

In hindsight, he now knew he should have probably stopped at the sixth beer, but it was too late for that now. He hadn't hit anything yet, and he was basically home. Daniel saw his house coming up and pulled into his driveway without much caution. About halfway up the driveway, he felt a bump on the right side of his car. He parked the car where it was and stumbled his way over to the right side of his vehicle.

Sure enough, just behind the front tire on the passenger's side was the crushed body of a cat. The cat's exposed organs glistened from the small amount of light coming from the streetlights close by. With a groan, he carefully pushed the body onto what was left of its back. He bent down and looked at the tag that was covered in fresh blood, hoping to see its name. He took his thumb and wiped off a bit of the crimson liquid to reveal the word, "Muffin".

"Great," Daniel muttered to himself. "It's Don's cat."

He stood up and looked to his right at the house that stood next to his. He checked his watch and contemplated what he should do. It was only eleven, but it was the middle of the work week. Daniel was sure Don would most likely be asleep by now. Though, he had really been meaning to talk to Don. He shrugged and started trudging across his lawn and onto his neighbor's.

"What's the worst that can happen?" Daniel said to himself. "He's already a total dick to me anyways."

He stumbled up the front porch steps to Don's house and sluggishly banged his fist against the door. There was a moment where nothing happened and then Daniel saw the light in the living room come on. The door swung open and he was met by Don's larger frame looking down at him.

"What the hell are you doing?" Don growled, "It's almost midnight you intellectual midget."

Daniel couldn't help but chuckle a bit at the insult as he leaned against the doorframe. He took in a deep breath, "It's about your cat, Don." He let out a small burp that wafted into his irritated neighbor's face.

Don took a step back and covered his nose. "Jesus Christ! You smell like an outhouse, you moron!"

Daniel moved his left foot a little into Don's house before continuing, "I ran over your cat." There was a moment of awkward silence as Daniel watched the fury build up in Don.

Then Don couldn't hold back and yelled, "You stupid, drunk pig! You drink and drive like a prick and run over my cat. Then you dare to just nonchalantly come to my house in the middle of the night and drop this news on me!"

The sound of someone coming down the stairs took Don's attention away from Daniel for a moment. He took a few steps over to the stairs and saw his wife about halfway down.

She asked in a confused voice, "Don, what are you doing up?"

Don replied in a tone just a bit above a whisper, "Our neighbor had some news for us that he decided just couldn't wait. I'll be back up in a minute."

Daniel took advantage of Don being preoccupied and took a few steps into the living room, and picked up a lamp. He ran towards his neighbor with the lamp raised then smashed it against his head. Don stood still for a moment then fell face-first onto the stairs.

Don's wife let out a scream of terror and took off for her bedroom. Daniel gave chase after he stumbled over Don's unconscious body. As soon as he reached the top of the stairs, he laughed to himself when he saw that she hadn't locked the door. He slowly walked into the bedroom, letting his eyes adjust to the darkness. He might have still been drunk, but he had been preparing for this for weeks. No matter what, he was going to make his plan work. Out of the corner of his eye, he saw something run towards him in the darkness. He was just able to step back in time to avoid being hit by something. He swung with a right hook and connected with the figure, who then hit the ground hard. Daniel flipped on the light switch and saw that he had knocked Don's wife unconscious. *Perfect,* he thought to himself.

Don awoke with a stinging pain in the back of his head and he felt as though all the blood was rushing to his head. His eyes began to adjust to the light and the first thing he noticed was that everything was upside down. He blinked a few times before he realized that he was the one facing the wrong way. That's when he finally felt his hands tied behind his back and his feet were tied as well. He pulled his head up to see that he was suspended from a rafter that was part of an unfinished ceiling.

Don looked to his right to see someone else also suspended off the ground with a bag covering their face. He looked around the place to see various tools and a table that was covered in empty beer bottles. He tilted his head downward and got a look at a plain, cement floor. It was then that he put it all together and realized he was in an unfinished basement. He heard the sound of someone coming downstairs and looked to see Daniel walk down.

Daniel noticed that Don was awake and a smile spread across his face. "Excellent! You're finally awake," he said enthusiastically, as he walked over to a corner of the basement. Daniel pushed some things around and then grabbed two metal troughs and dragged them across the cement floor. He paused for a moment, taking some deep breaths. "These suckers are heavy," he joked before continuing to pull them.

He pushed the troughs under Don and the other suspended person. Daniel walked over and took the sack off the mystery person to reveal the face of Don's wife. She let out a cry of terror as she glanced between the two men with a look that was a mix of horror and confusion.

Daniel clapped his hands together. "Now that you're both awake I can get this shindig going!"

He walked over to a workbench and picked up a large knife. Daniel walked back over and stood in front of the couple as they started to beg for their lives. Daniel studied the knife and drowned out the sounds of their pleas.

He finally interrupted by saying, "I didn't get a divorce." He let his statement hang in the silence of the moment, really savoring the quiet. Daniel continued, "I told everyone Chrissy and I divorced, but that didn't happen. I mean, do you really think she was able to move out of here in less than a week and not leave a single trace?" He looked back and forth between the couple as if he wanted them to answer his rhetorical question. He sighed. "Nope. We didn't get a divorce. I killed her."

Don's wife let out a cry. "Oh god!"

Daniel smiled, "Yup, hung her up from these rafters and slit her throat open like a pig. There was blood everywhere. Yeah, I had the trough to catch most of it, but man there was still some that got on the floor. I was cleaning up little specs of it for weeks."

Don said, completely horrified, "What the hell are you talking about?"

Daniel pointed his knife at Don. "My new hobby, Don." He walked over to the table with the empty beer bottles and proudly stood next to them. "You see," Daniel beamed, "I started brewing my own beers."

Daniel picked up one of the bottles and held it out so the label was showing to the couple. "I won't lie, in the beginning, I made some crappy beer. I didn't know what I was doing wrong, but I just could never seem to get the taste right. I was always missing something. That is, until I accidentally ran over a homeless person a few months ago." He slowly started walking back over towards the helpless couple. "I swear that it was an accident. I had never killed a person before. I knew I couldn't go to jail. So, I brought the body back here, cut it up, and buried it in the backyard. But before I buried it, I collected a lot of blood from it."

He crouched down between Don and his wife and looked back and forth between them with a crazed look in his eye.

"Yeah, that's right," Daniel laughed. "I put that hobo's blood in a batch I brewed up, and you know what?" He stood up and said excitedly, "That was what I had been missing! I don't know what it is, but blood is the key ingredient to make some tasty beer."

Don yelled, "You're crazy!"

Daniel shook his head in disagreement. "Not crazy, just an entrepreneur. You see, I started selling my brews to local businesses. I've been making a lot of cash off it. I mean, people really do not miss the homeless at all. It was going really well, till Chrissy found out."

Don's wife started to cry. Through her tears, she yelled, "You animal!"

Daniel shrugged. "I couldn't have her going to the cops. Plus, her blood made some of the best beer I have ever tasted. Tainted blood just really takes away from the flavor potential of a brew. That's where you two come in." Daniel pointed his knife back in forth between them, "I need more untainted blood, and Don, you've been a massive prick to me. I've always hated your guts." Don spit at Daniel, who casually sidestepped out of the way. Daniel smiled. "I truly hate you, Don. That's why I'm going to make you suffer."

Daniel quickly crouched down and brought the knife up to the throat of Don's wife. He took the blade and brought an inch of it across her throat. A large dribble of blood began to seep down the side of her face and into the trough. Don let out a scream of anger and thrashed against his bonds. His wife gasped out in pain and shock at what was happening.

With the knife still held in that spot, Daniel moved to where he was positioned behind her. "I moved so you can have a better view," he sneered at Don. "Now you can watch my work up close and personal!"

Daniel began to drag the knife slowly across her throat, opening it up as he went. A large torrent of blood poured out from the opening he was cutting into her. He gave one final quick movement, and the rest of her neck was opened. Don yelled in grief as he watched his wife go motionless. The life drained out of her as large quantities of blood poured from her open wound and over her face into the trough. He looked to see his wife's hair coated in the red liquid.

"Wow!" Daniel exclaimed. "She was a bleeder. There's already at least two gallons in there. It won't take long to drain her at all."

Don screamed, "I'm gonna kill you!"

Daniel stood up and in one fluid motion walked to Don and stabbed him in his gut. "No Don, I'm gonna kill you." He crouched down and looked him dead in his eyes. "But I'm not even gonna bleed you. This one is personal!"

Daniel drove his right hand into the open wound on Don's gut. Don screamed in pain as Daniel wriggled his fingers around in it. He grabbed ahold of something and pulled. Don let out screams of agony as Daniel slowly pulled out his intestines.

Daniel pulled out at least five or six feet with slow, tedious care. "I don't want any of this bad boy to break," Daniel whispered.

Don screamed in anger as loud as he could at Daniel, which sent Daniel into action. He took Don's intestines and wrapped them around Don's neck. Then Daniel pulled the bowels tightly as Don began gasping for air. Slowly but surely, Don started to flail around less and his gasps were becoming weaker. Daniel felt relieved by this, since blood had started dripping out of the opened wound and was starting to make his hands slippery. He was honestly finding it a little hard to keep his grip on Don's intestines.

Finally, Daniel watched the last bit of light leave Don's eyes and he released his grip. Daniel fell back onto his butt and watched as the intestines slowly flopped off Don's neck and into the metal trough. Daniel crawled back to Don's body and used the knife to rip open Don's throat. There was a small trickle of blood that started to come out, but Daniel knew it wouldn't be as much as it could have been. He didn't care. It had been so cathartic to strangle Don. It was worth it. He slowly stood up and inspected the floor before him. The ground within a four-foot radius of the bodies was covered in blood. He was going to have a terrible time cleaning up.

"Oh well," he said as he dropped the knife on the floor. "At least I'm gonna have one hell of a brew."

That'll Melt Your Brain

Christina lightly kicked the front door open as she struggled to carry all the groceries that were loaded up in her arms inside. She noticed her son sitting in the living room, playing on his computer. Christina yelled at him, "Jackson! Get off the computer right now!"

"Aw, why?" Jackson whined.

"Because you've been on it since you woke up," she replied as she quickly walked into the kitchen and sat down the groceries. She sighed deeply before saying, "It's not good for you to spend all your time looking at a screen. You'll melt your brain doing that."

He rolled his eyes at the cliché phrase his mom had just used. "Fine," he grumbled, "I'll be off in a second."

Jackson listened for the sounds of his mom unpacking the groceries. Once he heard them, he knew he would be good to keep messing around on the computer for at least a few more minutes. He went back to playing the strange game he had started before his mom walked in. Jackson was getting close to the end of it and just had to take care of the final boss. He frantically pressed the right combination of keys so his in-game character could avoid the devastating attacks that were being thrown towards it. After executing every dodge perfectly, he moved his character forward and delivered the killing blow.

"Yes!" Jackson blurted out in celebration.

He quickly checked to see if the outburst had gotten his mom's attention. When it was clear that she was still putting things away, he let out a quick sigh of relief. Jackson turned back towards the screen and noticed a popup message that had appeared.

He quietly read to himself, "Congratulations on defeating the final boss! Click here to claim your prize."

With a shrug, he clicked on the button to collect whatever award he was supposed to get. The computer screen suddenly went black and he sat there in confusion for a few seconds. After about a minute or so, he started to get frustrated with the computer. He was just about to start pressing the power button rapidly when he noticed something strange happening on the screen. The display itself seemed to be rippling ever so slightly, as though it had transformed into some sort of liquid.

He stared at the screen for a moment before tentatively reaching his hand out to lightly touch it. As soon as his finger touched the screen, a rippling effect shot out from the point of connection. Jackson watched the screen ripple before him with extreme curiosity. He wondered if this was the prize the game was talking about. Suddenly, the ripples just stopped. Jackson was about to touch the screen again when he noticed that something was poking out from the center of it.

He watched as some sort of object began to gradually come through the screen. Now, he was filled with more curiosity than confusion. He needed to know what was happening, so he continued to just sit there. A hand began to make its way out of the computer, and he noticed that it looked like it was composed of the same black, seemingly liquid material as the screen. Jackson suddenly realized that the hand was reaching out for him, and the feeling of curiosity was quickly replaced by paralyzing fear. He wanted to run away, but his body failed him and the un-natural limb drew closer. Suddenly, the hand shot forward and grabbed ahold of his face. An excruciating pain filled his head, but for some strange reason, he couldn't cry out for help. Instead, he could only tremble in reaction to the pain.

Christina finished packing away the last of the groceries. She turned back to the living room to find that Jackson was still focused on his computer screen. She shook her head as she walked up behind her son and poked him in the back. "Hey," she firmly said, "I told you to get off that thing. Do it now, or you're grounded." When he didn't respond she asked, "Do you seriously want to be grounded?"

She was losing her patience when she looked at the computer and noticed that the screen was blank. Christina found that strange, but was more interested in why Jackson still hadn't responded to her. She moved around the couch to where she was in front of her son and leaned down to look him in the eyes. Christina immediately noticed the blank look that covered Jackson's face.

She was about to ask what was wrong when she spotted something running out of his right ear. It was a grey liquid that periodically dripped from Jackson and onto the couch. Christina gently poked her son's left shoulder and watched as his head tipped further to the right. The grey liquid came spilling out onto the couch and after a moment her son's body fell over. She let out a horrified scream as she looked into her son's lifeless eyes, while his brain continued to spill onto the couch.

Ding-Dong Run

"I'M SO SORRY GUYS," Dante whimpered.

"It's okay, man," Hugo whispered.

"Be quiet!" Joel snapped. He scanned the near-pitch-black room for signs of movement. "We have to keep our voices down," he whispered. "Otherwise she's going to find us."

"Okay," Dante said as tears formed in his eyes, "I just didn't know she was real. It was supposed to be a prank. Just a little Halloween fun. How was I supposed to know that the Solomon Witch was real?"

"Look man," Joel turned to Dante. "You have to keep it together, or we won't be able to make it out."

"Foolish boys," a crackling, old voice echoed through-out the house. "There's no way you can escape me! Especially not on All Hallows Eve, when my powers are at their greatest!"

"Shut up you old hag!" Joel shouted, "We know exactly what you are, and we're not scared!"

A howl of laughter filled the air as the voice said, "Oh really? Let me guess, you think I'm the Solomon Witch? Margarette Solomon?"

"Well, yeah!" Hugo shouted. "That's exactly who you are!"

"A valid guess I suppose," the voice replied. "I've taken the form of Margarette, but I'm no witch."

"Then what are you?" Joel asked.

"I'm something far worse," Margarette cackled. After a moment she said, "I know your worst fears. The nightmares you dream about when you close your eyes. I can become horrors you couldn't possibly imagine."

"Why don't you show yourself!" Joel screamed in frustration.

"Because it's so much more fun to toy with you instead." Margarette's voice came from behind Joel.

He whipped around to see nothing but the doorway leading out of the living room and into somewhere that was shrouded in darkness. Joel turned to his two friends and said, "We need to stay together. She can't get us if we do that."

"Oh Joel," Margarette sighed. "Always playing the leader of the gang. Making your friends help do your dirty work… like burying the neighbor's cat."

"Shut up!" Joel shouted. "You don't know anything about us!"

"Oh, but I do," Margarette cackled. "I know Dante is a bedwetter." She paused to let it sink in. "Of course, he was too embarrassed to tell you. He's so passive that anyone can walk all over him. Hell, his own bladder defies him by emptying itself on his bed!"

Dante felt the others looking at him and started to cry. "It's true! I'm so sorry guys. I'm such a loser!"

"Hey, it's okay man," Hugo put a comforting hand around Dante. "You know we love you. We ain't gonna stop being your friends just 'cause you wet the bed."

Margarette noticed that Hugo's efforts to comfort Dante were working and she growled. "You really are something else, aren't you Hugo?" she rhetorically asked. "Your demons don't hide under the bed or change shape. No, they're the ones you have to live with. How hard is it to go home when your worst nightmare is waiting to chastise you?"

Hugo let go of Dante and took a few steps forward. "Stop!" he shouted. "Don't you dare say anything else!"

"How many scars?" Margarette asked. She chuckled at the silence. "There's really nothing else I have to ask. You feel pain every time you step into your house, so you fight your hardest to make sure others never feel the same. A pathetic response, from a pathetic human. All you humans are."

"You can't call us pathetic," Joel shouted, "You used to be a human!"

Margarette screamed, "No! I never was! I'm something far greater than that."

"Doesn't seem like it to me," Hugo yelled.

"I think it's time I stopped playing around," Margarette growled.

The floorboards suddenly creaked from above and the boys all looked up. They waited anxiously as feet slowly moved over the weathered wood towards the stairs. Dante couldn't help but tremble as he quietly sobbed. Hugo stood completely still as he focused on nothing else but the footsteps. He did this all the time at home with his father, so he knew exactly where Margarette was. Hugo heard the sound of a footstep on the top of the stairs and took a deep breath. Another footstep sounded, but it was right in front of the entrance to the living room next to where Dante was standing. Before Hugo could say anything, a pale hand swiped at Dante's feet and sent him falling to the floor.

"Help me!" Dante screamed in terror.

In a split second, he was dragged back into the dark as he continued to cry out for help. There was a loud snap and then Dante's screaming stopped. Hugo listened as he heard the sound of squelching and something wet being torn apart. He didn't want to think about what it was. After a few seconds, the disgusting noises stopped and the house was quiet again. Hugo strained his ears to hear where Margarette was. A footstep sounded from the archway next to Joel.

Hugo turned to Joel and screamed, "Watch out! She's right there!"

Joel sprinted forward and barely managed to avoid the sharp nails that slashed out of the darkness at him. He ran over to Hugo and turned to face Margarette as she slowly stepped out of the darkness. Her dirty and torn attire wasn't enough to hide the rest of her terrifying features. The boys watched as her completely white eyes seemed to move between them while her razor teeth gnashed together. She bent down to stab her sharp nails into the floor to show her power.

"Well done, Hugo," she sneered. "You've managed to keep your sociopath of a friend alive." Margarette chuckled, "I don't know why you would want to do something like that for someone like him."

"Shut up!" Hugo shouted, "I've had enough of your lies."

"My lies?" Margarette said in a hurt tone. "But I haven't told any lies." She pointed at Joel. "Ask your friend if that was the first cat."

"No!" Hugo screamed. He shook with rage as he stared at the stupid grin Margarette wore. After a few seconds, the anger began to dissipate and was replaced with curiosity. Hugo slowly turned his gaze towards his friend.

Joel must have noticed Hugo staring, because he said, "Please don't make me answer that."

Hugo shook his head. "I gotta ask."

Joel grimaced as he looked towards the floor. He hesitated for several seconds before whispering, "It wasn't the first."

"How many?" Hugo calmly inquired.

"Four, maybe five before that one," Joel replied.

Margarette howled with laughter. "See, Hugo! You've got yourself a little serial killer in the making as a friend. Some might say you would be saving lives if you killed him now." She took a step forward as she flashed her nails. "I know you're too kindhearted to actually do it, so let me help you."

Margarette lunged forward, but the boys managed to move just in time. Hugo took the lead and ran towards the stairs. He slammed his feet against each step as he sprinted upwards. He heard a thump from behind him and looked to see that Joel had tripped. Before his friend could get back onto his feet, the witch grabbed hold of his right ankle. Hugo turned back and started to descend the steps to try to help.

"Go!" Joel screamed. "Get out of here!"

Margarette pulled Joel down towards her and sunk her teeth into his neck. Hugo saw a spurt of blood come from his friend just before he turned away. He sprinted up the rest of the stairs and made his way down the hall. He tried the first door he saw and found that it was locked. Frantically, he continued to try every door he came across, but none of them would open. He turned to see the witch staring at him from the top of the stairs with a smile on her face.

"There's no way out, boy," she cackled as she started to slowly move towards him.

Hugo backed away from her until he bumped into a wall behind him. He turned to see a window peering out into the backyard. He scanned the ground below and saw that there was nothing but dead grass.

"You're weak," Margarette taunted as she closed in. "Just like all the others that have come here. You are all so easy to kill."

"If you think I'm weak," Hugo began to scream, "then you don't know a damn thing about me!"

Hugo turned and leapt at the window. The glass shattered against his weight and he found himself suspended in midair for a moment. In a matter of seconds, he fell towards the ground and landed feet first. He felt something snap in his left leg and crumbled onto the dead grass. Hugo let out a wail of pain as he gripped his broken leg. He turned over and looked up at where he had jumped out to see Margarette staring down at him.

It took him a few tries due to the pain, but he finally managed to pull the lighter he had taken from his dad out of his pocket. He slowly dragged himself over the grass towards the house. Hugo found a great spot where there was a small hole in the decaying wood. He flipped the lighter on and held it against the spot until he saw the flame latch onto the weathered material. Fighting against the agony, he dragged himself back from the house until he was at least fifty feet away. He looked back to see that the fire had already started to climb up the side and was about to engulf the window he had jumped from. Hugo could see Margarette screaming in fury at him as her haunt burned. He smiled as the flames danced.

Simply in Jest

LIAM CLIMBED ON TOP of the table and began to wildly flap his arms to mimic the process of flight. "Look at me!" he loudly proclaimed as his comrades watched. "I'm a mean old faerie, gliding over your houses. I be looking to shiv your wives and steal your dinner before ye even get off work!"

His mates burst out laughing and Liam grinned in accomplishment as he jumped down off the table. He puffed out his chest and took a small bow while his friends clapped in rowdy applause.

Their laughter was interrupted by Mr. McCarthy yelling, "Gosh darn it Liam! I thought I told you to stop climbing on the tables!" McCarthy pointed right at the rowdy bar patron. "Do that one more time and I'm throwing you out of here!"

"Oh, come on!" Liam protested, "I only did it so's I could do an accurate depiction of one of them shite faeries." He gave a wink to the aging bar owner. "I know you enjoyed it."

"You shouldn't be making fun of them anyways," a voice off in the corner of the tavern grumbled.

Liam turned to see Cillian sipping a pint at a tucked-away table by himself. There was an intense look on Cillian's face as he glared at Liam. The nature of the glare was lost on the inebriated patron, who responded to it by bursting out laughing. Liam slapped his hand against the table where his friends were sitting as he continued to roar with laughter.

"We got ourselves a faerie lover, boys!" he hollered in between gasping for air. He glanced at Cillian as he loudly asked, "So what is it about them that really gets you going?" Liam stifled his giggling for a few seconds so he could spit out, "The wings or the pixie dust?"

Roars of laughter erupted from Liam and his friends at the crass joke. Cillian didn't give any hint of reply, and instead, simply sipped his beer while glaring daggers.

Cillian waited for the overpowering noise to dip in volume before angrily saying through clenched teeth, "You should never make fun of a faerie."

"And why is that?" Liam inquired in a mocking tone. "Because I'd be making fun of one of your secret crushes?"

Cillian slammed his pint on the table as he growled, "Because they are wicked creatures with immense power!" He stood up from his seat and roared, "One faerie could destroy this entire town in an afternoon! They are not to be taken lightly."

Liam shrugged with a sigh. "I'm just playing around." He took a few steps away from his table before adding, "What I'm saying is simply in jest. I'm only joking Cillian. No need to get your nicely pressed pants all tied in a wad."

Cillian slowly lowered himself back into his seat before sternly replying, "A faerie doesn't care if you're joking or not. They'll tear you to pieces and leave your corpse to rot in the sun."

"I think that's quite enough morbid talk like that," McCarthy ordered as he wiped down the bar. "I don't want to hear any more gruesome stuff like that, or I'll throw you out of here!" he hollered as he pointed towards the front door. When Cillian didn't respond, the bartender slammed his hand on the bar and yelled, "Hey! Do you understand me?"

Cillian slowly lifted his head to meet McCarthy's gaze. He flashed the tavern owner an uncaring smile while scoffing at the threat that had been thrown against him. "I understand," he replied, followed by a brief pause before adding, "but it won't matter anyways."

"And why's that?" McCarthy inquired as a bit of apprehension started to bubble in his aging stomach.

"Because no one in here is going to be able to talk about faeries ever again," Cillian calmly responded as his eyes scanned the faces of the tavern's patrons. "Honestly," he shrugged, "Not a single one you will be alive here in a few minutes, so it doesn't really matter what I talk about."

"Is that a threat?" Liam growled as he balled his hands into fists.

Cillian turned his attention to Liam with a solemn look on his face. "I wish it was just a threat... but it's not."

"Oh really?" McCarthy said as he took his shotgun from its place just beneath the bar. He raised it up, pointing it at Cillian. "Because I feel you telling us that we're all going to be dead in a few minutes is the definition of a threat. Care to tell us how that isn't a threat?"

Silence filled the tavern as everyone sat in complete stillness. No one dared to take their eyes off the scene that was unfolding in front of them. Several more moments of painful silence crept by before McCarthy loudly cocked his gun to make Cillian aware of what he was doing.

"I wasn't asking," McCarthy growled. He yelled, "I won't stand for some drunkard threatening to kill me or my other customers. Get the hell out of my bar!"

"I told you," Cillian sighed and then took a large gulp of his pint. He set the glass down to finish the thought, "I wasn't threatening you." He looked McCarthy directly in the eyes as he said in a volume just above a whisper, "I was making you privy to the inevitable."

The look that Cillian was giving McCarthy heightened the ever-growing sense of anxiety that was now overtaking the old man's better judgment. His finger began to wrap around the trigger with his mind moving him closer to a decision he would not be able to take back once he made it. Suddenly, a loud thumping noise came from above, drawing everyone's attention towards the ceiling.

"What the hell was that?" Liam nervously gasped.

"Sounds like something hit the roof," McCarthy thought out loud. Despite his best efforts, his voice betrayed the sense of panic he was starting to feel. "Something big," he shuddered.

"Looks like they're here," Cillian whispered to himself.

"Who's here?" Liam desperately inquired. When he was met with silence, he raised his voice to repeat himself. "Who's here?"

Another loud thump came from on the roof, startling most of the those in the tavern. There was a collective gasp of dread made in unison by the patrons that further added to the tension. Almost all were either wearing expressions of concern or beginning to tremble in fear. All except for Cillian. He continued to casually sip from his pint while the others around him seemed to become more and more frightened with each passing moment.

McCarthy was fed up with the loud bangs by the time he heard the faint sound of wood cracking. "There's something on the roof!" he shouted.

Liam looked to the calm demeanor of Cillian and pleaded, "What's up there? You have to tell me!"

Cillian calmly set down his glass to reply, "I already did… you just weren't listening."

A loud ripping sound filled the room, causing several customers to shriek in surprise. Mere moments after the noise, a large ray of light that had not been there before seemed to land directly in the middle of the tavern. McCarthy traced the beam upwards with his eyes to find that a semi-large, freshly made hole in his ceiling was the culprit.

"I've had enough of this!" McCarthy yelled. He pointed his shotgun towards the area around the ceiling and fired off a shot.

After the initial screams from the shot faded, the tavern was covered in an eerie silence as everyone waited to see if anything would happen. The next few seconds that passed seemed like agonizing hours for most inside the walls of the tavern. Finally, breaking through the silence was a small and quiet chuckle. Everyone's attention moved towards Liam as he pointed a confident finger at Cillian.

"Looks like your inevitable isn't happening!" he spat out while continuing to escalate the volume of his uneasy laughter. "It was just an empty threat!" Liam shouted.

At that moment, one of the large windows at the front of the building shattered as an enormous object flew through it. The object rolled across the floor for a dozen feet or so before coming to a stop just a few feet from the bar. Everyone in close proximity to the thing wore a look of horror as they realized what lay before them. The thing that had just broken through the window slowly stood to reveal what it truly was, unfolding the blackened wings that stretched out to a span the size of two grown men. All stood motionless as the beast's fiery gaze scanned over them all. The creature let out a snarl as it showed its twisted and deformed face to everyone.

"What the hell are you!" McCarthy shouted in horror as he fired off a shot at the monster.

The blast tore through the creature's right-wing, sending inhuman flesh and buckshot into the nearby wall. Letting out a roar of pain, the beast turned its focus towards McCarthy. Before the tavern owner could properly reload, the creature leapt forward with purpose, easily covering the distance between it and the old man. McCarthy let out a small squeak of fear and then he was lifted off the ground. The beast hoisted him into the air, placing one hand on the top of the old man's head while the other held him in place. A light pull was all it took to rip McCarthy's head from the rest of his body, sending a spray of blood into the air.

Immediately, all hell broke loose as the patrons began to scream in horror. As the customers desperately tried to flee towards the doors, the monster bellowed out a terrifying roar that caused most to stop dead in their tracks. The second it had finished its call, several more creatures, very similar in nature to it, broke through the other windows into the building. The monsters swarmed the patrons, ripping them apart without a second's pause. With the screams of horror and sounds of flesh tearing around it, the creature twisted its mouth into a sinister grin. The thing turned its gaze towards the only person still sitting down.

Taking a quick hop over the bar, the monster landed just a few feet in front of Cillian. It stared down at him as its large figure easily towered over the man.

It slowly outstretched its hand and pointed a finger at Cillian. In a booming and warped voice, it growled, "You have done well by leading us here."

"It was my pleasure," Cillian responded as he cautiously lifted himself from his seat. He pointed to the set of tables that were a dozen or so feet from him. "The one who was mocking you is under there," he stated in a monotone voice.

"You bastard!" Liam screamed from his impromptu hiding place.

The faerie glanced at the table with a smile. "Excellent! Then our retribution will be swift." It moved over to the tables that Liam was hiding under while saying, "We will not be made fools of by a drunkard and an imbecile!"

The faerie easily grabbed ahold of Liam, pulling him from his hiding spot. Liam widely thrashed about in a feeble attempt to break free of the creature's grasp. With next to no effort at all, the faerie lifted him above its head. Pulling as hard as it could from both ends, the faerie listened as the man gave out a loud scream of agony while his body was torn apart. Entrails spilled out onto the floor as a spray of blood filled the air for a few seconds.

Cillian watched the faerie drop the fresh corpse to the ground before asking, "What will you do now?"

The faerie stared at Cillian for a moment and then casually responded, "We will level this town to the ground before moving on." It turned, spreading its uninjured wing while moving towards an opening in a window that had been created from the chaos. "I suggest you find a new home," the faerie sternly called out to Cillian. "We have spared you for now, but if we return to this place, I cannot guarantee that we will do it again."

With that, the faerie flew through the opening and was gone. The rest of its kind followed close behind, leaving Cillian alone in the decimated tavern. He scanned the room, truly surveying the carnage for the first time. The sight was worse than anything he could have imagined, and it easily left him overwhelmed in horror. He stood there in a state of shock while still being able to hear the screams of terror and chaos as they gradually grew farther and farther away.

In Her Father's Place

The darkness was as infinite as it was oppressive, reaching out to cover the entirety of the void. Marla sucked in a deep breath while trying to remain calm. She had been told about the blackness and how to handle it, but now that it surrounded her, all those lessons seemed futile. It felt like an oppressive force from some other realm was pressing down on her, though only just enough to make her uncomfortable and overwhelmed. She tried focusing solely on her breathing, but panic-stricken thoughts of what lay in the void rendered all efforts in vain.

Fear swirled around her, invading her mind and making it difficult to breathe. Finally, she could take it no more.

There was no point in remaining calm, so she took off in a dead sprint across the infinite plane of darkness. Surely there had to be some way back to the entrance she came through. She would find it and leave this hellscape behind. The fate of the village be damned. However, her desperate run was proving to be worthless as the darkness did not relent. There were no breaks in it, no sliver of light to be found. She was desperately fumbling about in an abyss that had no intention of releasing her. That fact was becoming more evident by the moment and the weight of the realization seemed to suffocate her.

Overcome by the bleakness of the situation, she finally came to a halt. Marla stared out at the nothingness of the void and screamed in frustration, "What do you want from me?"

She was taken by surprise when something answered, with a single word echoing around her. "Hello?"

"Is... is someone there?" she called out in response.

"Yes! Yes! I'm here!"

Marla desperately searched around her for any sign of the voice but encountered only darkness. "I don't see anything. I can't find you!"

"You won't find me with your eyes. Feel for me. Reach out with all your senses at once, it's the only way."

She didn't completely comprehend what was being asked of her, but she was eager to find something else besides infinite black, so she took the voice's advice literally. Marla closed her eyes and began to blindly feel about with her hands. These efforts only worked to heighten her desperation as nothing came of the endeavor.

"No! You must feel with all your senses!" the voice suddenly shouted with surprising intensity. The calm came back to it as it continued, "Clear your mind and focus all your energy on finding me. Do it and you will bring salvation."

Once again, she did not understand but followed the guidance. She took in a deep breath then tried to relax. Marla did her best to block out everything else, the fear, her confusion, even her own breathing, and focus solely on locating the source of the voice. Suddenly, something came into view at the limit of her vision. Nothing more than a speck on the horizon of the void, but it was something. She welcomed the break in the darkness regardless of how small it was. There was no time wasted as she immediately sprinted toward whatever it was, caution be damned. In a matter of seconds, it grew from a blip she could barely see to that of a grown person.

"I found you!" she gasped with relief upon reaching her goal. Their back was turned to her, but slowly they pivoted to reveal themselves to her. The face of a man she knew all too well greeted her. "Daddy?" she whispered, overwhelmed with confusion and joy.

"Babygirl, is that you?" her father asked in surprise.

"It's me! It's me!" she exclaimed as she wrapped her arms around him. "I didn't think I'd ever see you again."

Her dad chuckled while he kept his arms by his side. "You weren't supposed to."

Marla found that response strange and unnerving. "What do you mean?" she asked as she let go and pulled back a step or two.

"I came here willingly as the sacrifice so that no one from my lineage would be made an offering," her father explained. "That was the deal I made with the village elders. It would seem they have betrayed me."

"I... I don't understand. They told me... they said it had to be another from the Calgary family. They wanted Thomas but I... I couldn't let that happen."

Her father stared at her with an expression of immense sadness. She assumed this outward display of emotion was for her, but then he spoke. "They have lied to you, and me as well. In doing so, they have also deceived the owner of this realm. The master of the infinite void who keeps ultimate darkness from creeping into the realm of humans. It will not be happy with this deceit. Vengeance will be swift, and none in the village will survive."

"None?" Marla repeated in alarm. "What about Thomas and Mum? They did nothing wrong!"

Her dad shook his head, "The pact was clear when it was made seven centuries ago. The master will simply be abiding by the oath it promised to uphold." He took her by the shoulders and whispered, "I am so sorry, my child."

"Sorry? For what?" she inquired with a whisper.

"You are its companion now. It is you who will guide it from this realm to enact justice."

Marla shook her head in defiance. "No, I won't. I'm taking you and we're getting out of here."

He gave her a weak smile as the skin of his left cheek began to droop. "My life is done. I have spent a great deal of time as the just one's companion. It holds so much wisdom and power that a mere mortal could never begin to fathom its vastness. There are many things it has taught me, and for that, I am truly grateful. But the knowledge is too much for my meager body, as it was for my predecessors who served before."

Marla let out an audible gasp as the skin began to peel from the top of her father's forehead. She expected a geyser of blood to follow suit, but instead, sand came pouring out.

"My time is finished," her father said as he raised his right hand to show the skin falling off of it into the darkness at their feet.

She watched in abject horror as more of her father peeled away, revealing the bones that lay underneath. Finally, she could take no more and turned away, only to spot enormous tendrils slowly creeping forth from a distant space in the void. Her father's master, the one he had served for over a decade, had come to bid farewell to its faithful servant. She chose to look away from the ancient thing, bringing her focus back to what remained of her dad. At this point, he was a collection of bones that was somehow still standing, but the hardened material also began to crumble away.

"It will be good to finally sleep," her father's voice said from the open but unmoving jaw of the skull crumbling away before her. "I have been so tired for so long."

Answer the Phone

Thomas held tight to the cell phone in his right hand as he sprinted down the hallway. He frantically scanned the path in front of him for some sign of where Madison might be. Thomas saw a door up ahead of him to the left that seemed to shut just before he got there. He pressed his left ear against the door and listened for any sound coming from the other side.

Thomas held the phone to his ear and yelled, "Madison, are you in there?"

"Yes! I think I can hear you!" he heard Madison respond through the cell phone.

He hesitated, as he hadn't heard her voice coming from the other side of the door. Thomas took a deep breath before he started to turn the handle, finding that the door was locked. He banged his fist against it as he frantically yanked the handle in the hopes that it would open.

"Can you hear me, Madison!" he screamed at the door.

"Yes!" her voice said over the phone, but not from the room he was trying to get into.

He finally decided to move to a different room and tried the door that was adjacent to the one he had just been at. That door was locked too, but Thomas thought he might as well try to see if Madison was on the other side.

"Can you still hear me?" he yelled.

"I can!" Madison replied through the phone.

"Okay," Thomas nodded to himself. "I want you to start yelling as loud as you can. I think I'm close to you, but I won't know unless you make enough noise for me to hear."

"Let me give it a shot," Madison said in a desperate tone.

She let out a loud shout that easily hurt his ear with the phone being right next to it. He immediately brought the phone down near his waist and focused on trying to hear if Madison was somewhere nearby. After a few seconds of intent listening, he heard the faintest of yells. He quickly started to move back the way he came but course-corrected when he realized the shouts were getting weaker in the direction he was moving. Thomas took a few large steps down the part of the hall he hadn't explored yet and found that the shouts were getting slightly louder.

"Don't stop shouting, babe," Thomas said as he held his phone up to his mouth. "I can hear you."

He pushed forward down the hall, stopping at every door to see if the shouting was coming from the room on the other side. After six or seven doors, he finally realized that the yelling was coming from the room at the end of the hallway. He raced forward as fast as he could and desperately tried to open it. The handle was giving him trouble, but he could tell that the door wasn't locked. Thomas started slamming his body against the door while he kept trying to jimmy it open. After a few grunted efforts, the door suddenly flew open against his body weight and he stumbled into the room.

He quickly scanned the empty space for Madison, but there was absolutely no sign of her. Thomas heard a creaking noise coming from behind him and turned to see that the door was starting to close. He scrambled forward but wasn't able to stop the door from slamming shut. Thomas desperately tried to move the handle, but he could easily tell that it felt different from when he had tried to get into the room. The door was locked, and he was now trapped.

Thomas sighed in resignation as he held the phone up to his ear. "Honey," he quietly muttered, "I'm so sorry. I tried to get into the room that I heard you calling from but... I guess I was wrong."

"That's okay," Madison replied in a hoarse voice. "You just have to keep looking for me."

Thomas took a second before he reluctantly said, "I can't. I'm locked in one of the rooms."

"You just have to keep looking for me," she responded.

"I can't get out of this room, babe," he reiterated before adding, "I would if I could, but I don't think there's another way out."

"You just have to keep looking for me," Madison repeated in a deeper voice.

"I told you I can't!" Thomas yelled. "Are you listening to me?"

"You just have to keep looking for me," she once again repeated. Her voice was now much lower and seemed almost inhuman.

"What the hell is going on?" he desperately asked. "Why do you sound like that?" There was silence from the other end of the line and it quickly got under Thomas' skin. He felt his anxiety growing in the silence, so he cautiously asked, "Madison? Can you still hear me?"

"I'm going to get you," a completely different voice spat out.

Suddenly a loud shriek of static sounded over the phone. The noise sent a wave of agony into his right ear and he chucked the phone away. He immediately realized his mistake as he scrambled over and desperately picked up his phone. Thomas frantically checked the integrity of his device and found that he hadn't broken it. He let out a sigh of relief before he looked to see that his call with Madison had ended. Thomas redialed Madison's number right away and anxiously waited for her to answer.

After a millisecond of screaming static, a gentle voice answered with a timid, "Hello?"

"Maddie?" Thomas asked in confusion, "Is that you?"

"Madison's not here anymore," the gentle voice replied.

"What do you mean?" Thomas growled. "What did you do to her?" he yelled.

A different voice suddenly shouted, "Nothing compared to what's going to happen to you!"

The call immediately ended after that, and he desperately tried to call again. Each time he redialed Madison's number he received a message that told him that she couldn't be reached. His frustration built with each failed attempt and he eventually fell to his knees while screaming in anger. Thomas dropped the phone on the floor and slammed his fists against the ground. All he wanted to do was find Madison and get out of this hellhole, but it seemed like that was becoming more unlikely with each passing minute.

Thomas yelled at the ceiling, "Why are you doing this to me?"

The sound of his ringtone going off took him by surprise and he jumped a little before he realized what was happening. He stared down at his phone screen as it lit up with an unknown number. Thomas hesitated to answer and debated what he should do. He cautiously moved his hand down towards his phone before he pressed the button to reject the call. Thomas took a deep breath before picking up the phone and redialing Madison's number. After a few moments of anxiously waiting, he felt elation as he heard the sound of someone answering coming from the other end of the call.

"Madison!" Thomas sighed with relief. "I'm so glad you picked up. I've tried to call you at least five or six times."

"This isn't Madison," a gruff, low voice growled on the other end.

"Where is she?" he yelled, "What have you done to her?"

"You should've answered the call," the voice snapped back. It started a sinister chuckle before saying, "Because you didn't answer the call you've lost contact with her, and you'll never hear her voice again!"

"Lost contact!" Thomas shouted in confusion as the call ended. "Wait! What call?" he yelled.

Thomas realized that whoever had been on the other end, they hadn't heard his last question. He let out a whimper of defeat while his mind raced with all the worst possibilities of what could be happening to Madison. He couldn't help but start to pace the room he found himself trapped in. There was no way he was going to calm down as the fear that Madison might die continued to creep closer to the front of his mind. Finally, he couldn't take it anymore and ran over to the door and started slamming his fists against it.

"Let me out of here!" he yelled out. "If you lay a finger on her I'll kill you! Every last one of you!" Thomas started kicking the door as well while continuing to shout, "You've made the biggest mistake of your lives!" After a few minutes, he wore himself out and had to stop. He kicked the door one last time before he slammed his back against it and slumped to the ground. "Just tell me where she is," he let out in a feeble gasp.

Suddenly, his phone started to ring again. Thomas scrambled towards his phone that he had left sitting on the floor. He picked it up and looked at the screen to see another unknown number trying to reach him. A terrible feeling started up in his gut, and he knew he shouldn't answer it. He quickly rejected the call before trying to redial Madison.

"What the hell?" Thomas muttered to himself as he scrolled through his contacts.

All the names he should have been able to see were replaced by random letters that had been arranged into complete gibberish. He frantically scrolled down the list but ran into the same thing. Thomas continued to go up and down the list as he frantically searched for Madison's name in his contacts. He finally decided that he wasn't going to reach her by doing that and went into his recent call log instead. Thomas was met with a white screen which made it seem as though he had no call history.

In frustration, he cried out, "Why is this happening?"

No sooner had he finished saying that, than a text message popped up on his screen. It was also from an unknown number, but he was at his wit's end and decided to open it up anyway.

He peered down at the message and read out loud, "You didn't answer the call. Now you can't contact anyone. Don't make that mistake again."

His phone started to ring again with the unknown number from before. Even though whoever was holding him there had made it clear what they wanted him to do, he still felt the need to be defiant. His anger bubbled up inside of him as he thought about what the monsters were probably doing to Madison. Thomas scowled at the call lighting up his phone screen and rejected it once again.

"Go screw yourself!" Thomas screamed, before also shouting, "Let Madison go and then I'll answer your stupid calls!"

A sudden force slammed into the door, which startled him. He scrambled away as someone continued to bang against the other side of the door.

"What do you want?" Thomas yelled over the loud banging. "Why are you doing this?"

The thumping against the door stopped and he sat there in confusion mixed with relief. His phone started to ring again and he looked to see the same number as before. He stared at it for several seconds before rejecting the call. Immediately after he had done so, the banging on the door started up again. As he watched the wooden barrier shake and move with each hit against it, a worry that it wouldn't hold began to grow inside of him. He felt as though the door was shaking more with each passing second, and he truly didn't want to know what was waiting for him on the other side. Suddenly, his phone rang again, but this time he accepted the call.

"I did it!" he shouted. "I answered the phone. Now tell that thing at the door to go away!"

"No," the gruff voice on the other end bluntly responded. The pounding on the door stopped and the voice continued, "That's not how it works. You didn't answer the calls. You were given every chance, but it's too late now."

"Then why call again!" Thomas screamed in anger.

"Because this is the last voice you'll hear before you die," the voice sneered. "You've lost the privilege to speak with others... and that will cost you your life."

The call ended and he was left there with a horrible feeling in his gut. He slowly turned his gaze towards the door just before the pounding started back up. Thomas couldn't help but tremble with each blow that hit. After a few more strikes, some of the material from the door flew off onto the floor. He began to shake his head in denial as a hole started to form in the center of the door. Thanks to the hole, Thomas was able to see what was coming for him. He screamed in absolute terror at the abomination that would have him in its grasp in a matter of minutes.

A Violet Shine

It was on Maria's first day of work at her new job that she noticed the violet shine. Except, it wasn't so much a shine at that moment as it was a dull light that barely managed to seep out from under the locked door it was contained behind. Since her company had been growing much more quickly than expected, when she was brought on, they had nowhere to put her. This was why she had been placed at the very end of a hallway, in a makeshift cubicle with a locked door only a few feet to her back when she worked.

At first glance, the light was nothing to pay any attention to, it was just something that she noticed. However, as Maria continued through her first week at the company, she realized that the dull, violet light was always shining on the other side of the door. That was when her curiosity became piqued, and also when she learned that the door was locked. With a barrier in her way that she could not move, she decided to leave the curiosity alone. Yet, it continued to linger in the back of her mind as she worked, slowly taking up a larger chunk of her thoughts.

By the time she started interacting with her coworkers, Maria felt a connection to the dim light. After casually bringing up the door in conversation, she learned that the room was a mystery to most in the company. The door had been locked for well over two decades by the time she joined the growing staff, and no one could give her any answer for what lay on the other side of it. This only increased her curiosity about the situation, leading her to begin developing theories on what could possibly be generating the light. The gnawing notion that she didn't know the source of the illumination ate away at her. It drove her to the action of being the first person in the office every morning, simply so she could sit in the dark and just stare at the dim bit of illumination from the small slit underneath the doorframe. Her favorite part of the day quickly became those moments where she could be alone with just her thoughts and the violet light.

When she was four months into the job, she noticed the violet light coming from somewhere else. One of her coworkers, an older man who normally warmed his tuna in the microwave to the chagrin of everyone else, had the tiniest halo of violet wrapped around his pudgy frame. The sight of it greatly troubled Maria, as it brought forth many more questions that she could not answer. She spent days' worth of time lost in thought, trying to piece together why such a special aura would connect itself to an unimportant man. This puzzled her until the day of the man's retirement, which was also when the halo disappeared from around the elderly coworker.

The following morning, she noticed that the light escaping from under the door had grown just a little brighter. It was a discovery that excited Maria more than it should have for a person of sound mind. Regardless, just like the light, her drive to answer all her questions grew a smidge stronger. She decided to come into the office at an even earlier time, stretching the minutes alone in the darkness to well over an hour. All the while, she studied her coworkers from afar, hoping to spot the same violet halo that she had glimpsed before.

As time went on, the company continued to do well, which led to large shifts in positions. Maria was given a promotion and her pick of offices on her department's floor, yet she chose to stay in her cubicle instead, to always be in close proximity to the violet light seeping from underneath the locked door. Her coworkers began to take notice of her strange behavior, and in turn, they steered clear of Maria.

It took eleven months from the spotting of the first violet halo for the second to appear, but once she saw it, she was eager to add its illumination to the source behind the door. The second halo enveloped an intern by the name of Marco, a good kid by all accounts. She had nothing against him, but he was standing between her and the answers she so desperately wanted.

It was probably far too easy for her to find out the passwords to get into Marco's computer. And it was also too easy for her to delete every important file that had been entrusted to him. The poor intern hadn't even backed up his folders properly, making it all the more devastating when Marco logged back into his computer mere hours after she had completed her dirty work. The boy's internship was terminated at the end of the week despite his insistence that he hadn't deleted the files. Maria felt a twinge of guilt over what she had done to the poor boy, but that immediately evaporated when she saw the violet light shining even stronger from under the door.

Over the next two years, the violet halo appeared with greater frequency. As soon as she spotted the coworker who was encircled by the precious light, she would begin scheming on how to get them out of the company. Through her own brand of smooth-talking, Maria managed to get many of the illuminated individuals to take an early retirement, or leave the company of their own accord. For the coworkers who didn't bend to her words, she sunk to less savory methods. Various forms of blackmail and anonymous threats were certainly not beneath Maria in the pursuit of her goals. With each coworker that she expunged from the company, her methods became more immoral, while at the same time, the violet light continued to glow ever brighter from behind its solid, wood barrier.

Maria continued to come to the office earlier and earlier, which greatly cut into the amount of sleep she got. Yet, the sizeable decrease in rest didn't seem to bother her as long as she was near the violet light. It had become so important to her that when she was not in view of it, she did not feel whole. The light soothed her anxiety, and in turn, made her want to discover its secrets even more. Her isolationist ways became even more extreme, reaching a point where she would spend days without saying a single word to another human being. All the while, her efforts bore the desired results, with the violet light growing in intensity to the point of becoming a bright shine.

Then, the halos suddenly stopped appearing to Maria, leaving her with more desire than ever as the answers lay just within her grasp. She waited patiently at first, but after several months without sign of a violet halo, she began to lose control over her emotions. Her anxiety took an iron grip over her actions and she became prone to random outbursts that were quickly followed by mood swings. All the while, the violet shine consumed her waking thoughts. It reached the point where she just didn't leave her cubicle, she simply lived there. Maria slept under her desk, and due to her growing anxieties, she was only able to sleep for an hour or two each night.

By the time the final halo appeared to her, she was far past the point of no return. Her mind had all but eroded away, with the only things present in her brain, besides thoughts of the violet shine, being the simple knowledge needed to still do her job. So, when a violet halo appeared around Mr. Tholters, her boss, her thoughts all converged on one conclusion. Tholters was a middle-aged man who was decades from retirement, and far too in love with his employer to leave them. He was also a squeaky-clean family man who lived the ideal life with his wife and two daughters. This meant that all of Maria's normal tactics would not work on Mr. Tholters, which left her with no other choice but to take drastic measures.

That's why she waited until Mr. Tholters was working late one night before enacting her plan. She had spent the hours leading up to the critical moment sharpening her letter opener so it would be easier to penetrate the skin with. The first stab was off its mark and ended up landing in Mr. Tholters' left side. However, it was enough to draw blood and startle her boss into a temporary state of shock, which provided her time to deliver three more blows before he started to put up a fight. As the crimson blood poured from his body, it mixed with the violet halo, creating a new and beautiful color that made Maria weep from its beauty.

It would take sixteen total stabs before Mr. Tholters stopped moving, but she added seventeen more until the halo fully disappeared. With her horrific task complete, Maria sprinted back to her cubicle where a tsunami of realization slammed into her. For the first time in years, she actually felt remorse for all the horrible things she had done in pursuit of the purple shine. Her body trembled while her spirit unraveled as she replayed the monstrous actions she had committed over and over in her mind. The review of her transgressions was interrupted; however, by the clear sound of a door being unlocked.

That noise erased all the feelings of remorse inside of her and replaced them with feverish excitement. Maria scrambled to her feet to watch the door open on its own to reveal the violet shine in all its glory to her. The power of the illumination was far greater than she had imagined, and the sheer intensity of it began to physically overwhelm her. Maria's skin almost immediately began to blister and burn under the violet rays as her mind finally snapped from the awesome power displayed before her. She cried out in agony as the light took hold of her body and began to assimilate her into a part of the illuminated energy it was made from. In less than a minute, she had been completely absorbed into the violet shine.

Once the process was completed, the door slammed shut and locked, while the shine was reduced to nothing more than a dim glow. Upon discovering Mr. Tholters' remains, the office was shut down for several weeks before eventually reopening. Several months passed and then Draymond was hired to fill the position that had been left by Maria's disappearance. Of course, thanks to more unexpected growth, there were not many places to put Draymond. Therefore, he was given Maria's old cubicle to work in... right next to the locked door. It was on Draymond's first day there that he noticed the violet shine.

Another Man

SEBASTIAN GLANCED OUT THE back window of his taxi while nervously shaking his leg. He brought his attention toward his unlocked phone, which was opened on the past few text messages between him and his wife. He couldn't help but reread them even though they left him with a terrible sinking feeling in his stomach. His eyes were drawn to the picture his wife had sent of her in some rather promiscuous lingerie, but that wasn't the part that got to him. *I can't wait for tonight,* he read to himself for at least the dozenth time.

Any other time, he would have eagerly welcomed the message with open arms and anticipation, but not when he was on a business trip that was supposed to last for a few more days. There was no way that he would have been able to come home in time for a romantic evening, and his wife knew that. This left only two possibilities that would explain the strange text message. She was either sleeping with another man and had sent the message to Sebastian by accident or... he had come back. If the latter was true, then his wife's life was in danger.

The cab finally pulled to a stop in front of his house and all the energy that had been building inside of him while sitting in the back seat of the vehicle sprang forth. He haphazardly threw some bills from his wallet at the cab driver before scrambling out of the vehicle. Sebastian raced up the driveway of his house, taking note that there wasn't another car besides his wife's. This fact upset the horrible feeling in his gut even further, and he sprinted up the steps to his home. He frantically dug out his keys before unlocking the door and throwing it open. The door slammed into the wall, creating a small divot that he completely ignored as he scrambled inside.

"Babe!" he called out in desperate hope of a response. "Honey, are you here?" he shouted.

Sebastian bounded up the steps to the second floor of his house while continuing to call out for his wife. The silence that greeted him was worse than any other response he could have received. Despite desperately wanting to find his wife, he found himself pausing at the top of the stairs. He tentatively reached for the hall light while his eyes anxiously looked at the darkness that stretched out before him. Tentatively, he flipped on the light to find that nothing seemed to be out of place. The only thing that didn't seem right was the fact that the door to the bedroom was ajar, which was something that never happened.

In an instant, he felt his heart drop into his stomach. His hands began to shake as he forced himself to move down the hallway towards the bedroom. Every ounce of his strength was placed in moving step by step towards the open door. By the time he was halfway down the hall, he was able to see a small stain on the carpet just inside of the room. The color was difficult to identify at first, but after another step, he was able to identify that the stain was dark red. Sebastian's legs gave out as he fell onto his knees, gasping for air as his emotions overwhelmed him.

It took several minutes for him to calm down enough to shakily stumble to his feet and continue forward. Each step caused his heart to beat faster, as he was able to notice more of the little red stains covering the bedroom carpet. Sebastian finally reached the doorframe and used it to support himself as he hesitated to peer inside the room. He wanted to run from the situation and just pretend like it wasn't happening, but he knew he couldn't do that. Sebastian took his shaking hand and lifted it to grasp the light switch to the bedroom. He couldn't help but let out a tiny whimper as he flipped it on, revealing his wife's mutilated body lying on the bed.

Sebastian felt tears begin to well up in his eyes as he stared at the unmoving body that was his wife. Blood seemed to soak every inch of the bed, and there were cuts and gashes so deep in the body that it looked as though some of his wife's limbs had been completely severed. His attention was so devoted to the horrific display on the bed that he didn't initially notice the man sitting in a chair off to the left side of the room with his head pointed at the ground so his face would remain hidden. Sebastian didn't need to look to see who it was; he already knew the monster that sat in the chair. Yet, he looked anyway, forcing himself to come face to face with his wife's killer.

The man gave a slow and condescending clap as he gradually raised his head to reveal that he looked exactly like Sebastian. "I'm glad to see you finally made it home," he sarcastically said. "I was starting to get worried."

"You son of a bitch!" Sebastian screamed at his lookalike. "Why did you do it?"

"Why?" the man said in confusion. He thought for a moment before giving a small shrug, "I guess I just hate seeing you happy."

Sebastian let out a quiet whimper as he whispered, "It's not fair."

"Not fair?" his lookalike shouted as he suddenly stood up. He glared daggers at Sebastian as he ranted, "You know what isn't fair? Being you! And not just you... no... I had to be the worst parts of you. The outcast version that lives on the fringes of society because you're too busy living your perfect life to think about me!"

Sebastian's lips trembled as he replied, "I didn't ask for this."

"You think I did?" his doppelganger growled. "You think I wanted to be brought into this world through pain and hatred just to find out I was nothing more than a throwaway? A being dreamt up by a child's imagination and willed into existence molecule by molecule only to be forgotten?" The doppelganger pointed to the mutilated corpse on the bed and screamed, "You did this, not me!"

"How many people have you killed?" Sebastian spat out in disgust. "How many would still be alive if I hadn't wished you into existence?" He growled as he said, "I wish I never would have made you."

"Good!" the doppelganger shot back. "Because I don't want to be here. I never wanted to, but I can't leave now, can I?"

That response left Sebastian speechless, so he turned his gaze to the ground for a few seconds. All the regret that had followed him for most of his life came boiling back up to the surface. It tore at his insides, eating away at his strength until he told himself that all he wanted was for the nightmare to end. Sebastian glanced at his wife's lifeless body on the bed, causing a new wave of guilt. Overwhelmed by his emotions, he turned his attention away from the body and that was when he noticed the large knife sitting on the nightstand to the right of the bed, still covered in blood.

His doppelganger followed Sebastian's gaze to the knife and let out a chuckle. "Haven't we been through this already?" he asked while shaking his head.

Sebastian reconsidered making a move for a brief moment before racing over to the knife and snatching it up. The whole time, his doppelganger stood still, simply watching as Sebastian pointed a deadly weapon at him. There wasn't any fear in the copy's eyes as Sebastian tentatively made his way around the bed, making sure to keep the knife out in front of himself for protection. The doppelganger scoffed and rolled his eyes while Sebastian came to a stop just a few feet in front of him.

"You're not going to do anything," the copy sighed. "You've already tried, remember?" He took a small step forward, "Or did you forget that you were too much of a pussy to get revenge on the person who killed your best friend?"

At the mention of that incident, Sebastian's hand reacted by making a slicing motion through the air with the knife to force the doppelganger back. Instead, the blade just barely nicked the palm of the copy's left hand. That was enough to surprise the copy, causing him to reflexively take a step back as a small trickling of blood moved down his hand. Sebastian stared at the copy's wound before checking on the condition of his left hand to find the same injury had appeared.

"Well... that was something," the doppelganger said as he pressed down on the wound to stop the bleeding. He noticed that Sebastian had gone motionless with shock and couldn't help but comment, "I guess you had your moment of pretending to be a hero." When there wasn't a reply, the doppelganger continued. "We both know you don't have the sack to do anything else. After all, if you hurt me, it only ends up hurting you. And it's pretty clear that your life is just too precious to..."

In an instant, Sebastian lunged forward and plunged the knife deep into the doppelganger's gut. A look of pure shock spread across the clone's face as his mouth hung agape in pain mixed with surprise. Sebastian felt a shooting pain explode in his stomach, forcing a moan of agony to erupt from his lips. The doppelganger desperately tried to push Sebastian away with a trembling hand, but he couldn't throw back the original version of himself.

Sebastian felt his resolve start to slip, as the pain of the self-inflicted injury was far greater than he had anticipated. In a desperate attempt to strengthen his determination, he closed his eyes and thought back on all the people his doppelganger had hurt or killed. This reignited the rage he had felt towards his clone and he let out a scream of fury before ripping the blade out of his doppelganger's gut. He proceeded to ram the knife back into the abdomen of his copy, causing more blood to spill forth from the two of them.

"S-S-Stop it," the doppelganger pleaded.

"No," Sebastian wheezed out in response. He stabbed his copy again as a wave of blood traveled up his esophagus and forced its way out of his mouth. Sebastian leaned in close and whispered into his doppelganger's ear, "This... ends... now."

Sebastian produced one more stab for good measure before his legs gave out and he tumbled onto the floor. He lay there, taking in gasping breaths of air while he watched his doppelganger struggle towards the bedroom door. After only a few steps, the clone fell to the ground. The copy let out a couple of final gasps before growing completely silent and still. Sebastian couldn't help but smile before coughing up another wave of blood. He closed his eyes for the final time, drifting off in peace knowing that his doppelganger would never hurt anyone else.

The Squelchers

"GET AWAY FROM THE side, Enrique!" Captain Stargen screamed.

Enrique jumped in surprise before running away from the spot he had been standing in, on the portside of the deck. The waves slammed into the sides of the medium-sized fishing vessel, sending gallons of salty water onto the deck. Stargen looked out at the stormy horizon ahead of them and contemplated what to do.

"Captain!" Jay screamed, "We need to turn back! The storm's too great!

"We can't turn back!" Stargen shouted. "We're too far into the storm. It's better to head forward and hope to come out ahead of it."

Lu scrambled across the deck to secure the last bit of the catch they had made before the storm started. Jay decided to follow him and help. The two grabbed the net half-filled with salmon and started to drag it towards the holding containers. Using their combined strength, they managed to heave the net over the first container and started to dump the fish into it. A powerful wave hit the ship, knocking them off balance and causing them to drop the net. The two scrambled as fast as they could, and quickly recovered it. They finished dumping in the last of the salmon just as Enrique was moving along the portside of the ship again.

Enrique still didn't have his sea legs, so he had a bad habit of clinging to the rail as he moved about the ship. The boat was rocking far too hard for him to keep his balance without holding on. Jay saw Enrique moving along out of the corner of his eye and was about to tell him to stop when another large wave struck the starboard side of the ship. The wave was strong enough to rock the boat towards its portside. Enrique flew into the railing and lost his grip. He let out a scream of pure terror as he fell over the railing into the sea.

"Enrique!" Jay screamed in horror. He ran to where Stargen could see him and screamed, "Man overboard!"

The captain took his eyes away from steering and looked to see what Jay was talking about. When he noticed that he couldn't spy Enrique anywhere, he immediately knew what had happened. He scanned the horizon to see if there were any breaks in the storm. Way in the distance, he spotted what he believed was the edge of the maelstrom.

"Hold on for your life!" he shouted to his crewmembers. "I'm going full speed ahead to try to get us out of this storm!"

Stargen cranked the motor and revved the engine. The boat took off through the churning water as best as it could. It moved and bounced over the waves with more ease than before, but it was still facing great resistance as it progressed along. Stargen checked the dial for the engine and saw that he was taking her close to critical level. He looked in front of him just as a massive wave was rising up. There was no time to avoid it, so he had to try to ride the wave and hope the vessel wouldn't capsize. They moved up fifteen feet, along with the wave, before the boat fell off and slammed into the water. A massive amount of water spilled onto the deck. Some of it made its way down the stairs and below the deck.

The waves continued to churn and move as he steered the boat towards the edge of the nasty storm. He looked out and saw that they were but a few minutes from being out of it. Stargen pushed the engine a little bit harder, sending the water that had seeped through the wooden boards dripping into the motor. A puff of smoke began to bellow out onto the deck and the engine sputtered. He slammed his hands against his control panel and screamed. Thankfully, the storm was moving away from the direction they were going, so it would pass over them in a few minutes.

The captain made sure that the waves were starting to die down before making his way below deck. As soon as he turned to the engine, he saw the large pool of water surrounding it and cursed. He went back up to be greeted by Jay and Lu, who silently stared at him. He sighed deeply before delivering the news. "The engine is busted."

"What do you mean 'busted'?" Lu demanded.

"The damn thing took on water that had washed down from the deck." Stargen sighed, "Looks like we're going to have to float for a little bit."

"So, we're stuck out here!" Jay shouted. "This is great!"

"Hey!" Stargen snapped, "I don't like this any more than you." He shook his head. "Especially, since we're in prime Squelcher territory."

"What did you just say?" Jay asked, "Did you just say... Squelcher territory?"

"That I did," Stargen nodded. "You mean to tell me you've never heard of the Squelchers?"

Jay laughed, "No, no I have not. From the way you're talking, I take it it's some sort of sailor tale."

"Don't knock the stories told by sailors," Stargen warned. "They exist for a reason. No matter how outlandish they are, there's always a bit of truth to them."

Jay rolled his eyes. "Well, are you going to tell me about the Squelchers or what? I assume you're going to ramble on about them regardless of what I say, so you might as well get it over with."

Stargen shot Jay a glare before starting, "I'll tell you about the Squelchers alright. Just to warn you." He cleared his throat. "Squelchers aren't like other creatures from sailor folklore. Everyone knows what a mermaid or the Kraken looks like, but no one knows what a Squelcher looks like."

"Then how did the stories of it get started?" Jay asked in a condescending tone.

"Because of the awful noise they make," Stargen fiercely said. "It's this horrible, wet sucking sound. I guarantee it's not like anything you've ever heard before. It's like stepping into a spot of fresh mud and getting stuck in it. When you try to get out, and it makes that suctioning sound. You take that times ten, and that's the closest thing you can compare to the noise those creatures make."

"Don't tell me you've heard them before, Captain," Lu said with a look of horror on his face.

"Aye, I have." Stargen shook his head. "I was starting out on a commercial fishing boat. There was an accident with the netting on our latest catch and I cut up my hands pretty bad." He took in a deep breath before continuing, "I was below deck when I heard this horrible sucking noise against the wall of the ship. I had never heard anything like it. I would be a liar if I said it didn't terrify me. I stayed below deck, too afraid to go investigate what it was. Even when the screaming started, I didn't leave the cabin." He looked at Jay. "When the noise finally faded away, I went to check on my fellow shipmates... and I found I was the only one left. A twenty-man crew and I was the only person there."

"You're a lucky man," Lu said quietly.

"I didn't feel lucky while I was floating there by myself for three days. The Coast Guard finally found me on the third day. I was barely clinging to life, but they managed to get me out of there before I died." The captain pointed at Jay. "That's why you should be worried. We're right in their territory." Stargen gestured at the waters around them. "All the encounters where people like myself have survived, the Squelchers have only shown up in this part of the waters."

"So you could point out where the Squelchers are on a map?" Jay asked.

"I don't need a map!" Stargen yelled. "I can tell they're in these waters. It's a feeling I've had with me since I heard them. It can't be explained."

"So why did you lead us here then?" Jay asked in an accusing manner. "If it's so dangerous, why didn't we go somewhere else?"

"It was this or the storm!" Stargen shouted. "We already lost Enrique to it. I didn't want to lose any more men."

"How valiant of you," Jay said sarcastically.

He turned away and looked out at the waters. They had calmed significantly since the storm passed them. The boat was barely rocking as the ocean breeze blew over the deck. If they were stranded out here, at least the weather was finally nice. Jay was about to apologize to the captain when he heard a strange noise. It sounded like something wet was slapping against the bottom of the boat. A bit of apprehension rose up in him at the thought that he might have just heard one of the sucking sounds Stargen had described.

"Did you hear that?" Jay asked.

"I didn't hear anything," Lu replied.

"Be quiet," Stargen said as he strained his ears to hear.

After a few moments of silence, Stargen shook his head and started to walk to the navigation room. Jay relaxed and was about to chuckle at the fact he had let the captain's stupid story get to him. A second sound came from the starboard side of the boat. This one was far louder and clearer than the last. A wet sucking noise, like nothing Jay had heard before, sounded again. The panic inside him grew as several more sucking noises came from the sides of the boat. He looked to see Stargen frozen with fear as they both listened to the noises.

"They're here!" Lu screamed. "The Squelchers have come for us!"

A moment later a pale hand shot up and grabbed the railing on the portside of the boat. Everyone stared in shock as the hand pulled a human face up and into view. The dead eyes of Enrique stared off as he pulled himself up and over the rail. Each move that Enrique made was accompanied by the disgusting sucking noise. Jay looked at his deceased shipmate and noticed there was color missing from him, and not just his skin. It was like the sea had begun to wash the tones off his clothes as well as his body. When his body flopped face-first onto the deck, he also no-ticed that it looked like Enrique's skin was more malleable than it should have been. The dead sailor raised his head, and Jay looked at a face that had been flattened to the side.

Several more hands started to appear on the railing of the ship. Jay began to slowly move towards the stairs that Stargen was standing on. Several Squelchers pulled themselves up over the railing and landed on the deck of the ship. They were completely white creatures that seemed to be made out of clay. He could tell that they were once men, because they had some shape that resembled the form of one. One of them lifted their head, and Jay could have sworn it was looking at him. The eyeless thing moved its head to follow him as he took a step.

Feeling a rush of terror come over him, Jay ran the rest of the way and shouted to Lu, "Run!"

He saw Lu sprint across the deck towards him. The Squelchers noticed too, and moved at incredible speeds. They swarmed around him with their disgusting sucking sounds and covered most of his body with their grotesque flesh. He screamed out in fear as the conglomerate of the Squelchers dragged him towards the railing on the portside.

"Help me!" he cried out in fear.

Jay barely had time to take a step down the stairs before Lu was pulled overboard. Dozens of sucking noises sounded in front of Stargen and Jay as the Squelchers advanced towards them. The two men climbed up the stairs and locked themselves in the navigation room. They trembled in horror as they listened to the sound of wet sucking against the door. After a few minutes of hearing the continuous noise, Jay noticed that the door was looking a little warped. He stared at it for a moment before realizing that the door was losing its color.

"They're wearing it down!" Jay screamed in terror.

As soon as he finished screaming, the door slowly bent forward and folded onto the ground, as if it had been turned into a giant thing of playdough. The creatures moved into the room and quickly swarmed them both. The Squelchers wrapped themselves around the men and dragged them out. Jay felt a burning sensation throughout his body that made it seem like his insides were melting. He saw that the Squelchers that were wrapped around him were approaching the railing, and he screamed as loud as he could. Then he was tossed over the side into the water. The Squelchers stayed wrapped around him as they sunk into the depths.

Forested Whispers

Bolton stopped moving and let the wheelbarrow drop from his grasp. It fell to the forest floor with a soft thud that barely even registered for him as he gasped for fresh air. Sweat poured down the side of his face, and he could feel the salty liquid forming over most of his body. He took a glance at the long-sleeved shirt he had on and observed that his sweat had soaked through a good portion of its surface area. There was no doubt that his pants were in the same boat, but he wasn't too concerned about that for the moment.

The exhausted man bent over, placing his hands on his knees while he continued to gasp in deep breaths of fresh air. There was an aching that rippled across his legs, and Bolton couldn't help but feel some anger towards the ground he currently stood upon. Thanks to the recent bout of rain, the soil had become far more malleable than normal, which in turn caused his wheelbarrow to frequently find itself stuck in the ground. He had been slowly progressing through the forest for several hours, with more time spent prying his wheelbarrow free from the muck than actually gaining any ground.

After taking the time to catch his breath, he stood up straight and leaned in towards the enormous pushcart. He gently pulled the grey tarp off to check on the woman who had been placed inside. Bolton gave her a few pokes before letting out a small sigh of relief upon confirming that she was still unconscious. He stared at her for some time, his mind wandering off to someplace far away from the forest he currently found himself in. It didn't take long for a group of soft voices to begin whispering inside his head. The voices quickly grew in volume while maintaining the tone of a whisper. This snapped his thoughts back to where he was, and to the task he had yet to complete. Yet, that didn't stop the whispers from continuing to assail his mind, their volume rising to such a point that it brought pain to his mind.

"Please stop," he mumbled with the first tingles of un-pleasantness moving across his brain.

Bolton's request was met by the voices exponentially growing in volume, turning themselves into the equivalent of jet engines revving directly next to the poor man's head. A cry of pain erupted from his lips, which broke the relative tranquility that had been present throughout the forest a few moments prior. He squeezed the palms of his hands against his ears in a futile attempt to drown out the cacophony that brought such agony to his brain.

"I'm doing what you ask!" Bolton cried out. "Please stop it!"

Suddenly, all the voices ceased and he was met with silence once more. The jarring change took him by surprise, and he reacted to it by falling to his knees with an overwhelming sense of relief. He gasped in shallow and jagged breaths while his appendages trembled. Once his body had adjusted itself, Bolton slowly pulled himself from the dirt and brought his full attention to the young lady in the wheelbarrow. Though he was sure that everything was still in order, his anxious mind forced him to double check anyways. As he scanned over his abductee, he couldn't help but once again be drawn in by her natural beauty. It was the first thing he had noticed about her.

"You must really be special," Bolton whispered in an uneven tone, "since they made me travel so far to get you."

To simply say that he had traveled a long way for the unconscious woman in the wheelbarrow was certainly an understatement. After all, he had crossed through twelve different states and traveled over two thousand miles just to find her, an act that Bolton had done at the bequest of the disembodied voices that whispered into his mind. Though he pretended to have a choice in the matter, deep down he knew that the voices would have broken him, like so many times before. That was why he had just learned to accept the fact that he was but a humble servant of them. Nothing more than an agent acting on behalf of forces far greater than himself.

With them whispering into his mind, Bolton had completed dozens of tasks at their bequest, and in turn, the voices had passed large quantities of knowledge to him. They had taught him how to make restraints, completely crafted from the plant life of the forest that he lived in. There were lessons in creating sleeping agents from simple herbs and fauna that could be made so potent a grown adult might be placed in an unconscious state for days. One of said sleeping agents was the sole reason that Bolton's new abductee hadn't woken hours ago with cries of terror. Of course, he would have never needed to drug her in the first place if not for the whispers.

They were a ubiquitous force in Bolton's life and had been for the past several months. Slowly creeping into his brain at first, but eventually, they overtook all other priorities to become his sole focus. Though it did not seem like it, the arrangement had been beneficial for both parties. The voices gained a physical form that could carry out their important work for them, while Bolton felt that he was wanted, no... that he was *needed*. Being needed by another was a situation that he had not experienced for quite some time, so even if the feeling was delivered by disembodied voices, he still eagerly accepted it.

After a few more minutes of rest, he was finally able to get back to the important duty he had been tasked with. Bolton brought forth all his might and began to push the wheelbarrow forward once again. The weight of the abductee's body continued to push the front wheel of the barrow into the mud, but he was not bothered by it as much anymore. He had found a new sense of strength in those few moments of rest and was able to push forward with far greater results for his efforts. It took roughly two additional hours, but he finally closed in on the place he needed to be.

A familiar clearing eventually entered Bolton's line of vision, and he realized his goal was in sight. There was but one more eager push made by him before he broke through the thicket of trees. He wheeled the abductee about a dozen or so feet into the clearing and then came to a stop. Bolton gently lowered the wheelbarrow, a gesture of respect to the great presence he found himself in the company of. He took a brief pause to catch his breath, as well as wipe the droplets of sweat from his brow, before shambling around the pushcart and moving a few feet in front of a set of evenly spaced willow trees.

"I have done what you asked," Bolton wheezed out. He gestured with his left arm at the wheelbarrow. "She has been brought to you."

Good, the voices softly whispered in unison through Bolton's mind. *You know what must be done now.*

"Of course," Bolton replied while gasping for a breath of fresh air.

He glanced at the pushcart out of the corner of his eye and couldn't help but think about the tingling pain that already flowed through his legs. The act of pushing the wheelbarrow alone had taken so much out of him, Bolton seriously doubted if he could complete the rest of his work. The willows must have picked up on his hesitation, for their unorganized whispers filled his mind in an instant.

This simple strategy drove him to his knees, once more in pain, while proceeding to push all hesitation from him. Just as soon as they started, the voices stopped, and he was allowed to scramble to his feet.

Bolton immediately set to work by grabbing the wheelbarrow once more and moving it to where it was directly in front of a freshly made hole. He had dug the shallow hole four days prior and had grown worried that the rains would have destroyed his progress, but he was happy to see that the small pit was as he had left it. He fished in his pockets for a few moments, before pulling out a vial of the sleeping agent he had administered to the abductee days prior. For the next part of his task, he had to be sure that the woman would not wake up. The idea of the young lady regaining consciousness in the middle of the process he was about to undertake sent a shiver down his spine while creating a feeling of repulsion in his gut.

A small needle puncturing the skin of the unconscious woman was all it took for him to administer another dose of the sleeping agent, thus freeing him to complete the next step in the process. He grabbed hold of the woman's arms and tried his best to pull her from the pushcart without dropping her to the ground. Bolton struggled with the woman's weight in his arms, but he was eventually able to lower her onto the wet mud in a gentle manner. There was a small pause he took where he prepared himself, more mentally than physically, for the procedure he would need to perform as he pulled his instruments free from the wheelbarrow.

Bolton sat his tools gently onto the ground as he knelt beside the legs of the unconscious woman. He took in several quick, shallow breaths to pump himself up while he pulled his hunting knife out. Gently, he used the blade of the knife to cut the young lady's pantlegs up to her knees so he would have an unobstructed view to complete his work. The blade was then lowered to the point where the tip was barely touching the skin, a few inches above the ankle. His hand trembled as he lightly poked the woman's right leg. He drew the blade away and checked to find, to his relief, there was almost no blood flowing from the wound. The last thing he wanted to have happen, was for the young lady to bleed out before he could complete what needed to be done.

Now that everything was where it needed to be, he began his work. The first cut was always the hardest for him, and this time was certainly no exception. He had to force his hand to carefully push the blade fully into the skin. Once the first incision had been made, it was fairly easy for him to move the blade around the appendage, slowly cutting a neat line as he went. Bolton repeated this process on the other leg, and he moved a little faster, seeing as one of the appendages had already been opened up. He was once again thankful for the sleeping agent, as a nice side effect of the concoction was that a person's blood thickened, making it harder for someone to bleed out.

Regardless, he still had to move quickly. He leaned down to where he was a few inches away from the cut he had made on the incapacitated woman's left leg. Bolton then proceeded to slip the fingers of both of his hands into the cut on opposite sides of the appendage. With a strong, but careful pull, he began to meticulously take the skin off of the young lady's leg. He ran into a bit of trouble with the ankle, but he quickly resolved the issue and completely removed the outer organ. Immediately, he repeated the process with the right leg, revealing the muscular tissue of the woman's appendage.

Excellent, the willows whispered, *now plant her roots.*

Hesitating for a moment, he reluctantly took his fingers and placed them on the freshly skinned legs. He felt along the appendages until he was able to recognize the shape of the interworking of blood vessels. Bolton proceeded to focus his attention on a single vessel, as he meticulously pulled it free from the rest of the appendage with as gentle a touch as possible. Once he was successful, he continued the unnerving process, pulling dozens of vessels away from the unconscious woman's legs. Blood started to flow more freely with each new vessel he worked on, which caused him to slow his process more and more thanks to a growing sense of anxiety.

Eventually, Bolton felt that he had done enough and stood up as he wiped as much of the crimson liquid off on his pants as he could. Not wasting another moment, he took hold of the young lady's arms once more and dragged her body in such a way that her feet ended up falling into the hole he had dug days prior. He then took a few moments to double-check that the area of the woman's body with removed skin was below the top of the small pit. Once this was confirmed, he quickly pushed the pile of mud he had left days earlier into the hole, and maneuvered the earth about so that it went up to the abductee's knees.

The manic energy of being close to finishing his project filled Bolton with excitement and he moved with a fanatic eagerness. He quickly gathered up a wooden cross he had fashioned weeks prior and moved to place it just behind the filled-in spot. Once he was confident that the cross was secured enough in the ground, he hoisted the incapacitated woman to a standing position and placed her back against the wooden object. He undid the plant-made bonds that had restrained her and used them to secure the young lady's arms to the cross. This left the abductee in a position very similar to that of a scarecrow, minus the fact that her legs were halfway buried in the ground.

Bolton stepped back and took a few moments to double-check his work before finding it to be satisfactory. He wiped another bead of sweat from his forehead as he turned his attention to a spot near the edge of the clearing, where his first bit of work stood in line with many others. Slowly he began to meander down the row of fifty or so people, all in various stages of their transformations. As he passed by each person, he could easily identify the plant-like features that had started to overtake otherwise normal-looking people. The skin of those further down the row had hardened and changed in color, making it more akin to bark than anything else. Some of the abductees had started to grow flora from their bodies or sprout tree limbs. All these mutations were proof that he had done his work correctly, and he couldn't help but beam with pride at his accomplishments.

Eventually, Bolton reached the end of the row and gazed up at the first person he had abducted. Of course, by this point, they were far closer in nature to a tree than a human being. The transformation led to rapid growth, causing the abductee to stretch to well over fifteen feet in height. Hundreds of tiny branches had sprouted all over the body, with leaves covering large chunks of the additional space.

Though the general shape of the abductee had been left intact, they had all but been remade into something completely different.

Bolton brought his gaze up to the enormous head perched atop the new creation. He couldn't help but be fascinated by the fact that though bark-like skin now covered the being, some facial features from what the abductee once was, still remained. Suddenly, a rustling began to sound, which was quickly followed by the eyes of the creation snapping open. It surprised Bolton to see that the eyes were made of flesh and not crafted in the image of a tree like the rest of the creature's body. The thing turned its gaze down to meet his stares and the two stood still in complete silence as they each studied the other.

You have done well, the willows suddenly whispered inside his mind. *We have enough now to take our revenge on those who seek to destroy us. They will pay,* the whispers growled, *for cutting down our brethren and using their corpses for nothing more than profit. The first one of our creations is now complete and ready to distribute justice.*

With that, the enormous mutation began to slightly move the appendages on its sides that had once been arms. It was clear that the wooden features made the limbs stiff and hard to move, but the creature eventually was able to flex them with relative ease. A series of creaking sounds accompanied each movement of the new being as it continued to loosen itself in preparation for the travel it would have to undertake. Bolton continued to stand still, completely mesmerized by the beauty of the thing. He did not feel threatened by the creature that towered over him; in fact, its presence seemed to calm him more than anything.

The creation continued to loosen its form for several more moments before turning to the task of freeing its legs from the ground. Bolton remained still while the creature shifted and moved the ground right in front of him. For some reason, the sensation of calm that hung over him had continued to increase with each passing moment, pushing him to relax even further. Finally, the creature was successful in ripping one of its legs free from the ground, sending large chunks of mud and rock into the air. The mutation brought its appendage down onto the soil with a loud thud that was powerful enough to cause Bolton to stumble backwards for a moment.

The pheromones are working better than expected, the whispers mused. *They will be too relaxed to even process what is happening until it is too late.*

After a few more seconds, the creature ripped its other leg loose from the ground and was now able to move freely. Yet, the thing stayed put, staring down at Bolton with its enormous eyes of flesh and blood. A bad feeling began to bubble in the pit of his stomach, but the pheromones being secreted by the creation overpowered his anxiety and kept him from fleeing. The mutation slowly bent down, where it snatched up Bolton and lifted him towards its face. His mind completely comprehended what was happening, but despite his instincts to fight, he remained limp in the creature's grasp.

The time has come to strike down mankind. They have had their time to dominate this world, but now it is ours. There was a pause in the whispers before they filled Bolton's mind once more. *Though you have served us well... you are still one of them. So, we are afraid it is time for your end.*

"Wait..." Bolton quietly mumbled. "You can't do this."

Before he could protest any further, the creature closed its hand around him, squeezing with all its might. The sounds of cracking bones filled the air as he gasped out in agony, while the air was forcibly expelled from his lungs. Broken bits of bones punctured vital organs and skin across his body, allowing blood and viscera to freely flow from inside of him. The mutation kept squeezing until a final, loud pop sounded. It then opened its hand inch by inch, then turned the appendage over, allowing Bolton's lifeless body to fall to the forest floor. The corpse hit the ground with a loud thud that was quickly followed by silence. After a few moments, the monstrosity thundered forward in the direction of the nearest settlement of humans to dole out justice, while Bolton's corpse lay in the wet mud, surrounded by his creations. He would make an excellent fertilizer for them.

Holiday in Cambodia

Cole made it to the massive chain-link fence surrounding the compound's perimeter. He caught his captors with their pants down, dozing away in the middle of the night instead of keeping watch. There was a moment of hesitation as he reached out toward the barrier without knowing what awaited him. The metal could be electrified, or there might be a hidden alarm that would trigger when touched. Either way, if it led to his death that would be better than staying in that labor camp for another day. The things he had witnessed over the past few weeks had fractured his mind to the point where his sanity only hung on by a thread.

Flashes of horrific acts being carried out on his fellow forced laborers gave him resolve and guided his hands to gripping the fence. He waited, expecting something awful to occur, like his body exploding into a million pieces, but nothing did. The sweet absence of sound met Cole and nearly made him weep. Without wasting another precious second, he began scaling the chain link, but found his movement created a great deal of sound as the metal parts clanged into themselves. Driven by fear, he froze halfway up, terrified that the commotion had alerted someone to his escape attempt. There came no response from the night, so he decided his anxiety was just getting the better of him and continued the climb.

His movements were erratic and lacked any thought to them, driven off pure desperation. He frantically grabbed for anything above his head, then pulled himself upward when he found a holding. It took a few missed attempts and slips but he finally reached the top of the fence. At the peak of the barrier, there was nothing to stop him from climbing over. No additional obstruction such as barbed wire or strategically placed spikes. Cole didn't ponder why there was such lax security; his only focus was on escape, so he eagerly flung himself onto the opposite side of the barrier without a second of thought.

Unfortunately, he was a tad bit too zealous to cross over the top and lost his holding. His body fell to the ground feet first, impacting it with a rather loud thud. Thankfully, he had enough instincts to tuck and roll, so he was spared from the brunt of the mistake, but there was still pain to be felt. A searing ache exploded up from his feet and traveled to his knees in an instant. Once his body stopped tumbling through the dirt, Cole clutched at his hurting appendages while clenching his jaw shut with all his might. He desperately wanted to let out a wail of agony, but had the foresight to know better. Instead, he gave out a cry that was almost entirely muffled by his closed lips.

Though he certainly didn't have the time to do so, he spent a minute or two writhing on the ground until the pain subsided enough for him to stumble to a standing position. His initial steps were shaky and he almost fell, but somehow barely managed to keep upright. There was a bit of a limp as he broke into a labored jog, thanks to his left foot still recovering from the fall. In addition, that same appendage was showing the beginning stages of trench foot, no doubt brought on by the constant wet climate he had been forced to labor under. Regardless of what affliction he was dealing with, he pushed onward; he had to. His life hung in the balance as he stumbled over the uneven terrain of the tropical jungle.

Cole tried to keep his sole focus on covering as much ground as quickly as possible, but strange noises coming from the foliage surrounding him kept grabbing his attention. He had never heard such strange and alien sounds before. This terrified him and filled his thoughts with grotesque images of bizarre creatures that could be the culprits of such weird noises. A part of him wondered if the reason that no one was patrolling properly tonight was because the creatures hidden in the dark were the real security. No need to keep a close watch on the laborers if the native animals could prevent any escape to the outside world.

The incident of his leg becoming caught in a vine broke his train of thought away from the surrounding creatures, just in time for him to faceplant into the dirt. Searing pain and blood poured from his scraped knees, but it was just the thing to get him to focus properly. The moment he got back on his feet, he was honed in on finding a way out of the dense jungle. He picked up his pace from a mild jog to a full-on run. With him in the right headspace, it was significantly easier to weave out of the way of the various foliage and obstacles that came into his path.

Unfortunately for Cole, his body was not in as great a position as his mind finally was. Weeks of malnutrition caught up to him rather quickly and his energy rapidly drained away. His captors certainly did not feed him well. The laborers only received one meal a day, a bowl of rice. At least, he hoped that's what he had been shoveling into his mouth without any thought. Though that was enough nourishment to keep him upright during the taxing work of the day, nothing was left by nightfall. His body probably couldn't carry out a full-blown escape on such meager rations, but he had to try.

Despite his mind pushing him to physically keep going, Cole's body was not up to the task. Gradually, his pace decreased back to that sluggish jog he had initially started with. His limbs were also not responding to the commands given to them, with his legs only possessing a limited range of motion. Whenever a root or some foliage came up in his path, he would see it well ahead of time, but there was nothing he could do. His body simply wouldn't move out of the way, so instead he plowed through each minor obstacle.

Very quickly his breaths became labored as his lungs burned with agony to the point where he honestly thought they were going to rip apart. Muscle spasms in his legs sent constant jolts of hurt coursing up into his groin, causing him to let out audible gasps every one or two strides. He couldn't last much longer, but thankfully, he spotted a clearing through the dense cluster of trees. That sparked a touch of hope, which willed his limbs to stay together as he crossed the unforgiving terrain. He focused on that opening in the foliage, his eyes constantly watching as it grew ever closer. As he neared, he noticed several strange shapes just outside of the jungle. They were skinny in nature with something round toward the top of each one, but he couldn't identify them.

He didn't find out what they were until he exited into the clearing. In an instant, a moment that should have been joyous turned into one of abject horror as he found the strange shapes to be a series of heads mounted on spikes. The row of carnage spread out in both directions, stretching far beyond his field of vision. If there was something in his stomach Cole would have barfed, but instead, he dry heaved with so much force that he was driven to his knees. Thankfully, there was sand there to cushion his landing so his attention could be kept on violently hacking up air and spittle. After a minute or so, he managed to stop dry heaving long enough to wipe the globs of spit from his chin and take in the area surrounding him. It was a tropical beach in such pristine condition that even in the middle of the night he could identify its natural beauty. Unfortunately, he could not enjoy the paradise, but maybe one day, if he managed to survive, he could relax on a beach similar to it.

Cole pulled himself up from the sand and stumbled toward the waves gently rolling onto the shore. Way out in the distance, he could make out the shape of something massive. His best guess was that it was an island, roughly a couple of miles away. A swim of that distance would be near impossible for most, but he had more skills than the average person. He had done water polo in high school and college, so he had been an incredibly strong swimmer. Even in his underfed state, there was a chance he could pull it off. It was a slim chance, but he was willing to take the gamble. So, he continued to stagger forward over the sand that shifted under his weight as he mentally prepared for the arduous journey before him.

When he was but a few feet from the water, a sudden bang rang out, and instantly a fiery inferno of pain erupted on the right side of his torso. He glanced down at the afflicted area and noticed a sizzling hole cutting through his gut. Immediately, his body locked up from the unbearable pain while his knees buckled. He hit the ground, landing on his right side. Sand poured itself into the wound, but his mind was too overwhelmed with agony to even let out a grunt.

"Damn Zed! That was a hell of a shot!" came an excited voice from somewhere down the beach. "How the hell did you manage that in the dark?"

The person whom Cole assumed was Zed responded, "Oh, it's nothing with these new puppies that they got us. It lines up the shot for you if you know how to do it right. You're going to have to get pretty familiar with these bad boys, newbie. After all, patrolling this beach is most of the job."

"I know, you're right. I've just never been very good with firing them, but I'm sure I'll get it down."

Cole listened from his completely helpless position as the sound of two sets of footsteps moving over the sand grew closer toward him.

"So, I'm still a little confused on why we have to kill anyone who comes on the beach. There's nowhere for them to go, and if they tried to swim for it, they'd drown for sure," the newbie posited. "What's the point?"

"Good question, with an easy answer. We can only afford to cloak this place up to the shoreline. The second one of these bastards gets into the water, the coalition would be able to spot them, and that's the last thing we want." Zed sighed. "For some reason, those uppity assholes think they need to save every inferior species that exists. Waste of time if you ask me."

The newbie took a beat before asking a follow-up question, "If there's so much risk, then why use them? Why not just hire work like normal?"

"Two words: free labor," Zed replied with a chuckle. "You don't have to pay people you abduct, and nothing is easier to abduct than a human. Especially the rich ones. All you have to do is reach out to them saying you're giving them a free vacation to Cambodia or Laos, or some other place on Earth they know absolutely nothing about, and they'll willingly show up by themselves, ripe for the taking. It's really too easy sometimes."

"So, what's so special about those places? Is there something important in Cam... Cambo, whatever the hell you called it?"

The two came to a stop right in front of Cole and he was able to get a look at them. Even in the dark of the night, it was easy to make out their multicolored skin covered with random lines and patterns. That's all he needed to see to realize they weren't of his world and that he wasn't on Earth.

"Beats me!" Zed answered with a laugh. "But that part doesn't matter. As long as we can trick these dumbasses, we could say any place we wanted to. Now let's take off this fucker's head and put it with the others."

Cole saw the alien looking down at him and managed to make eye contact with the otherworldly being. His body finally unfroze itself, but all he was able to do was emit a wet, gurgling sound from his throat that caused the two extraterrestrials to jump.

"Oh shit! It's still alive!" Zed exclaimed, as it pulled a gun-shaped device out and pointed it at Cole. It paused, then looked to the newbie. "What am I thinking? You probably need the practice. Would you care to do the honors?"

"With pleasure!"

About the author

Radar DeBoard is just a simple horror writer, living in the bleak state of Kansas. Recently, he has grown weary of the limitations of his craft when it comes to scares. Sure, he has terrified many thanks to having eleven published books to his name as well as being featured in dozens of horror anthologies, but the fear from those stories wears off. He wishes to create something so horrific that it lingers in the reader's mind for years to come. Creating something of such unfathomable terror would cement him in the brains of those who purchase his books. Plus, it would be like he left a piece of himself in each copy of his work. A small bit of himself that can grow and watch, waiting for the right time to deliver a final fright.